CRAZY ABOUT YOUR LOVE

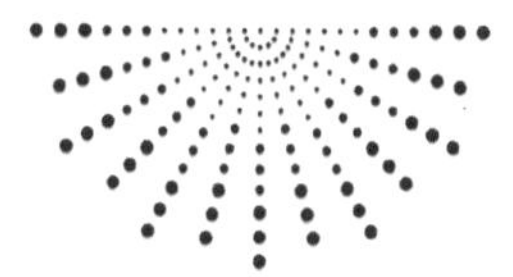

CHANIQUE JONES

SYNOPSIS

How do you love again when you're broken? When everything you've desired, prayed for, and imagined comes to an unexpected halt, picking up the pieces and moving forward seems impossible. How can one start over if they don't know where to begin? Twist, turns, pain, and confusion can lead you down the wrong path and you never know if you'll end up in the right or wrong hands.

Lee fell in love at hello, never knowing what true love was until it was too late. Every woman has a breaking point as well man, but will it be enough to start all over again?

Coby is your perfect man, everything you can imagine in one. Falling in love with Lee was something he never expected and he's willing to do whatever it takes to keep her.

Going through so much, in so little time causes their love to grow stronger with every milestone. Everything seems perfect, until things unexpectedly take a turn for the worst.

Trying to hold on and fight for a love that appears to be so perfect can drain you. Everything that glitters isn't gold, and the illusion you see from outside isn't always reality. Is love enough to conquer all and defeat the odds? Lee holds on until the very end and Coby isn't willing to give up the fight. When you're in love you do some crazy things never expecting it to cost you your life.

ACKNOWLEDGMENTS

Of course, I have to start by thanking God without him all of this wouldn't be possible. There were nights I felt like giving up and writing wasn't for me, but I continued to push and give it my all. With the motivation from my son Ke-Chan along with my family and friends I am happy to say I completed my fourth book in less than a year. Something I never imagined myself doing but I did it. I don't want to make this long and drawn out so I'm going to keep it short and simple. Thank you to all of my fans and supporters. I appreciate all the love you give me. I will continue to try my hardest to entertain yawl through my work and gifts. Last but certain not least I would like to thank my Publisher Shan! You are an amazing person and I want to thank you for giving the opportunity to be a part of this team #Shanpresents. I hope everyone enjoys this book just like you did my first series (No Love Given). Keep a look out for what's next! Thanks, Care Sincerely Chaniqué J.

LEE

irst let me start off by introducing myself, my name is Lanice Johns, but everyone calls me Lee for short. I'm 19 years old and far from your average young woman. I stand 5'6, weighing 145 pound, small waist pretty face as I like to call it, I'm a perky 36 c, nice round basketball booty, brown skin with light brown eyes, the perfect set of teeth thanks to my years of braces and retainers, I rock my hair in a short cut and many say I would put you in the mind frame of the female rapper Dej Loaf. I just recently graduated from high school and plan on attending college this fall at West Virginia University. Receiving a full ride scholarship for basketball is the only reason I chose to go so far away from home because I can honestly say I love the city life, especially my city. I was born and raised in Columbus Ohio, unlike many these days I grew up in a two-parent home and pretty well off. We weren't rich but we were far from poor. I'm the youngest of the three children my parents Yolanda and Larry have. There's my older brother Kris, my older sister Renee then me Lee the baby. My siblings and I are all two years apart and grew up very close. Although my parents raised us all up the right way, we all have minds of our own, my brother has been hugging the block since the age of 16 and my sister is a stay at home mother of one. My parents aren't happy about the way my siblings turned out, but they accept and love us all no matter what our life choices.

I'm currently in a relationship with my boyfriend Coby whom I've been with now for a little over a year. Coby and I met last year at the end of Spring it was Grad night at Kings Island in Cincinnati, Ohio. Although I wasn't a senior because my birthday falls late I felt the need to go considering I was already eighteen, plus of the girls I hung with a couple of them were graduating and so this was something they wanted to participate in for their senior year. Of course, since it was a Grad event there were seniors from all around Ohio coming to participate in the event. I was with my girls; Erin, Netia, and a few friends from our school when a group of niggas approached us. The purpose of them approaching us was so the guy by the name of Tye to kick game with Netia, long story short they exchanged numbers and we soon found out they too were from Columbus. When we returned to Columbus Netia had made plans to meet up with Tye of course he said his friends would be present so Erin, and myself tagged along needless to say. That night we all met up Coby approached me, and we've been pretty much attached at the hip ever since.

Coby is Dark skin with a chocolate complexion, about six feet tall, 260 pounds solid a perfect mixture of fat and muscle, big brown eyes that memorized me whenever I looked into them, with the cutest smile, Coby reminded me of Rick Ross without the facial hair and with a fade instead baldy. Coby is my big teddy bear; he is two years older than me and had already Graduated from high school and in his sophomore year of college. Coby is currently a quarterback for the Ohio State university, but he doesn't allow that to go to his head thank God, Lord knows I can't handle no ignorant cocky ass nigga. I won't say that he's not a ladies' man or doesn't have a group of fans, because he definitely is and does have them flocking to him especially since he actually gets field time and doesn't ride the bench. I don't allow the extra attention he receives to bother me because Coby treats me so well and doesn't have a problem letting it be known I'm his lady. I was still a virgin up until I met Coby, he didn't know I was and that's because of course I never told him. With Coby being two years older than me I didn't want him to feel like he was going to take my prize passion and run with it, so for that reason alone I kept it a secret. I told him that I had one sexual partner prior to him, and he was happy as hell about that, he claimed that it was rare for that to be true by the age of 19. I can't lie, me and all my girls were a little wild and kicked it just like any other group of young girls our age but we all either had only one sexual partner or were virgins up until recently. Any ways going back to the topic at hand; my man Coby he is the sweetest guy any girl could ever ask for and I can honestly say I love him with all my heart, he is the first man I have ever loved come to think about it. Yeah, I've been in several relationships throughout my years in school, but they were all short lived and lust or what I would call puppy love. Everyone including my parents love Coby, shit how could you not he's a charmer and the perfect gentleman always putting me first.

My older sister Renee and I were at Party City grabbing up a few last-minute items for my going away party. My parents had been going all out and we were having a big cookout for me going away to college since I was the first and only of their three children to be doing so. I can't lie the closer and closer it got to me leaving home the more nervous I got, but it was nothing I wouldn't be able to handle. After grabbing a few more tablecloths, packs of plastic cups, and "Party Here" signs we were headed back to my parents' house to help finish setting up. Soon as we were pulling into the driveway my cell phone began to ring and I already knew who it was by the ringtone. "All Eyes on You" by Meek Mills featuring Chris Brown and Nicki Minaj warned me my baby was calling. "Hey boo" I cooed into the phone greeting Coby. "Hey babe, what are you doing? Are you excited about your party?" Coby greeted me with the same amount of excitement in his voice to speak with me as I did with him. "Renee and I just pulled up to my parents' house from grabbing as few last-minute items. I'm bout to go in here and help my mom finish setting up. Yeah I'm excited but not more excited than I am to see your face later." Coby let out a light chuckle causing me to laugh as well. "I can't wait to see you either Pooh, go ahead and help your mom out and I'll see you later" "Ok boo talk to you later Love you!" "Love you too Pooh" We ended the call just like that. I loved the nickname Coby gave me "Pooh" I also loved the way it rolled off his tongue. That man makes every part of me smile from just hearing his voice.

"Lee snap out of it and help me grab these damn bags with your love-struck ass" Renee started talking her shit as always, bringing me back to reality. I knew we had pulled into the driveway but I hadn't realized she was now out the car and carrying the bags into the house alone while I was still sitting in the front seat of her 2011 Royal Blue Nissan Altima staring down at the screen of my phone smiling. "Shit my fault Renee, my bad I'll get the rest". "Trick I know you getting the rest shit I grabbed the majority of it". We were both laughing because she was telling the truth I was definitely love struck thanks to my boo and there was no denying it.

The aroma hit my nose as soon as I walked into the front door. My stomach started growling instantly when the scents hit my nose, I wanted to drop those bags right in the Livingroom and go grab a plate right then and there. I knew my mom was throwing down in the kitchen as she always did. My mom would put any women to shame when it came to her work in the kitchen there was no competition hands down. She taught me a thing or two growing up, but I knew my skill level would never amount to the damage she could do. My mom was out in the backyard setting up the tables with food while my dad continued to do his thing on the grill. The menu for tonight was off the hook. There was everything you could think of or desire eating available. Ribs, Grilled chicken, Fried chicken, Brats, Hot dogs, hamburgers, Grilled steaks, meatballs, Fried Catfish, Baked Macaroni and Cheese, Green beans, Corn on the cob, Greens with smoked turkey legs, baked beans, potato salad, macaroni salad, lasagna, my mom's famous five-layer nacho dip, dinner rolls, garlic bread, salad, cheese ball, veggie tray, fruit tray, cheese cake, pound cake, and a few different pies. There were three tables alone used for food only, and if anyone planned on bringing dishes of their own items there wouldn't be any room left. Right beside the food table was a table designated for drinks. We had two large coolers one filled with Ice and bottle waters, and the other held ice with a variety of cans including pop as well juice. It wouldn't be a black function without liquor so of course there was a table set up like a self-serve bar with mixed drinks and beer. All the top shelf liquor was kept inside the house in hopes no one would get too carried away. The center table that was decorated with yellow and blue tablecloths, and balloons held My cake displaying my kindergarten picture and my senior picture side by side. My sister even made sure there was a table set up for me to sit with a chair decorated especially for me and a card box for all my guests to put any type of gift cards, greeting cards or money into for me. Looking around at all the tents, tables and decorations set up I couldn't help but smile at all the hard work and preparation my family had done just for me. After finishing up the final touches I told my mom I was heading upstairs to get dressed before my guest started arriving.

I hopped out the shower oiled down with my favorite fragrance from Victoria Secrets Pear Glaze, while dancing around my room to the music I could hear playing from the DJs speakers in the backyard. Looking in the mirror and checking myself over I couldn't help but toot my own horn. "Damn Lee you bad" I said to myself. Dressing down didn't look bad on me; the skinny leg Rock Revival Jeans that fit all of my curves, matching Rock Revival fitted V neck tee, and Nude Christian Louboutin pumps fit the occasion well. I didn't want to overdo it with jewelry so I only wore my class ring, the 2 caret diamond bracelet my parents purchased me for graduating, my .5 caret diamond heart necklace that was passed down from grandmother, and a pair of 1 caret heart shaped diamond earrings that just so happen to be my favorite pair. Makeup was never really my thing, plus my skin was flawless so there really wasn't any need for it. I feathered my cut with my fingers making sure my hair was still slayed from my early morning appointment that I had today. I puckered my lips and apply one coat of Cremesheen Glass by MAC and made my way downstairs to join my guest.

I wasn't surprised to see my entire family accompanied by many of my friends from school, neighbor friends, my girls, and a few unfamiliar faces that I'm sure were friends of family or friends that just came to eat. The amount of people in my parents backyard would put you in the mind frame of a block party. I was happy to see that my going away party was about to be jumping. Thank goodness our home had a big enough space to occupy so many with a fenced in backyard that held a large swimming pool, basketball court, patio, deck, and fire pit. My parents said we were expecting anywhere from 150 to 200 guests so there were enough tables and chairs to occupy about 250 just in case, from the looks of it their estimate was damn close. The DJ was playing a mixture of hip hop and R&B from the 90 up to current music and was setting the mood just right.

"Hey beauty, how does it feel to finally be grown and soon to be on your own?" My brother walked up and kissed my forehead. He stood back and looked me over with a smile on his face. I could tell my big brother was extremely proud of me because it was written all over his face. Like any other day my brother wasn't alone, accompanying him were his two best friends: Dupree and Dame. Dupree and Dame both greeted me with a hug and kiss on the cheek and forehead as well.

"Hey Kris! For your information I been grown for over a year now news flash in case you didn't know I'm 19 not 18, but I can't lie I am excited to be out on my own" I smiled giving Kris an "I'm grown yet playful" attitude. Kris let out a chuckle and shook his head. Dupree and Dame walked off to enjoy the festivities with everyone else when they realized this conversation was about to be one of those heart to heart sibling things. Even though they were just like my brothers they allowed Kris to have his moments with family when necessary.

"I'm the oldest and you are my baby sister, you think I don't know how old you are? And 18 don't make you grown, so 19 sure as hell ain't too much of a big difference. Just cause you out on your own don't mean you can spend a night with your little boyfriend either. I bet not find out you down there turning out of I'll be shutting that whole damn campus down and you know I will so don't try me." Kris was always more overprotective of me than Renee and I knew that was only his way of showing he loved me and wanted nothing to happen to me. I also knew Kris meant every word he said and wouldn't think twice about making a trip to West Virginia to set me or anyone concerning me straight. For some reason Kris always referred to Coby as my little boyfriend even though he was only two years younger than him, I think that was his way of subliminally disrespecting him. Kris never really spoke on how he felt about me being in a relationship with Coby but I could tell he wasn't too fond of him or our relationship, but he promised not to bother us as long as Coby kept a smile on my face. I don't think Kris wanted me with anyone, shit leave it to him no nigga was good enough for me, I think he just feared I would get treated like he treated his females which would cause him to have to interfere.

"Well sorry to bust your bubble Kris but the law states differently, I've been grown since 18. You don't have to worry about my behaviors, I'm not trying to lose my scholarships playing around, but you know I wouldn't mind you coming to visit me. I'm going to miss yawl. This will be the first time I've been that far away from you guys and it won't be like just an overnight thing." I guess Kris could see that I was a little scared about leaving my family and going away to college, so he pulled me close for a hug and kissed my forehead again.

"Listen beauty you never have to be scared. I know you will be fine and if I thought you wouldn't be, I would be moving right down there with you. Shit plus I know you can hold your own unlike Renee scary ass so I'm not even worried. Shit you know I'm only one call away and I'll be there before we end the call " Kris made a joke about Renee knowing I would laugh to change my mood and walked away. Renee wasn't as scary as Kris made her seem to be, but she was definitely the lover and not the fighter out of the three of us. Shit there were times I fought Renee's battles, she's such a peacemaker it's ridiculous sometimes, but Kris is a hot head and never thinks twice so of course she would be scary to him. I'm the perfect medium of the two. I'm no killer but I'm far from a punk.

My night was going perfect. I had eaten so much, and the party was nowhere near being over. Shit I was still waiting on Coby to get here. My girls Erin and Netia were sitting on opposite sides of me eating and talking about Dupree and Dame. I knew Erin had a thing for Dame for years, but she always made a joke about it or pretended she was only joking. Shit Erin was grown so if she did talk to him it was between them two. Right as I got up to head over to the drink table to get me a bottled water, I saw Coby heading in my direction. Coby was matching my fly and it wasn't even planned. Coby had on a pair of vintage looking Rock Rival Jeans and shirt to make with a pair of white on white air force ones. His presence made my night! It's not that I doubted he would come but him actually being here just made me smile all over. Coby waved and gave a few head nods to people he knew as he passed them while walking my way.

"Pooh, you look amazing! And I see you were peeking through my window when I laid my clothes out this morning" Coby reached in and grabbed my waist and pulled me in close for a hug, although I knew he wanted to tongue me down we never did those types of things in front of my parents out of respect. "Thanks boo! you looking fly too I must say! Yeah so what I may have peeped through your window for a second or two but that's okay cause I look damn good on your arm matching your fly." I said giggling while grabbing his arm and heading over to the table I was sitting at prior to his arrival.

"What's up Netia, Erin?" Coby greeted them both

"Hey Coby" They both said in unison and went back to the deep conversation they were having eyeing a group of guys from our school. Erin scooted over a seat to make room for Coby so he could have a spot to sit next to where I was sitting.

"Babe you want something to eat I was headed to get me something to drink when you walked in." I asked Coby

"Hell, yeah put me a little bit of everything I haven't ate all day anticipating your mom's cooking yet still trying to make weight this coming weekend" Coby stated and pulled his chair out to have a seat. I gave Coby a sneak peek on the cheek and simply stated "I'll be right back". Coby licked his lips and smiled at me before I headed over to the food table to make his plate.

Walking over to the food table I was stopped by my crazy ass aunt Ginger, but everyone called her Gin for short. Aunt Gin is my mother's younger sister only being five years older than my brother

Kris. She was one of the young aunts that you loved to be around until she had one too many drinks. Aunt Gin looked like a younger version of my mother just light skin. Standing 5'5', weighing about 150, small frame she didn't have much when it came to ass or titties but that didn't take away from the fact, she was a damn twelve on a scale of one to ten. Her beautiful Coco skin complexion was flawless, with light brown slanted eyes, a small button nose, full lips, high cheekbones, and long jet-black silky hair that she inherited from my grandma. My mom always told us she earned her nickname early on from her favorite drink back in the day Gin and Juice. Shit she had graduated since then, now she no longer had a favorite beverage, anything that would impair your judgement after a drink or two she gratefully accepted. "hey baby I'm so proud of you! I just want you to know that no matter what your aunty is here for you and you know I'm going to be cheering you on every step of the way" "hey Auntie, and I know! What you go in that cup of yours" I asked her because as always, she had a cup in her hand that she was holding for dear life. "Girl you already know it's only juice with a spike or two" She started giggling like a young schoolgirl. Whenever she said just a spike or two, I knew it was more like three or four or possibly even her third or fourth cup with spikes in it. "Well make sure you don't have too many more cups of juice, I don't need you tapping out on us it's still early, and we turning up all night" It was almost nine o'clock and I knew that the party wouldn't be ending any time soon considering although some people were leaving there were still handfuls walking into the back yard for the first time this evening. "Oh hunny please believe me I'm not your mom already warned me I was close to my limit for the night and I couldn't crash on her couch" We both started laughing because we both knew every family function that took place over our house somehow some way Aunt Gin would end up either being escorted home because she was too drunk or passed out on our couch. "Ok we going see, well let me get over here and make these plates I'll talk to you in a little bit" "Ok baby get back to what you were headed to do, I'm about to go have a seat and chop it up with Renee's ass for a second". My aunt turned and walked away, and I proceeded to make Coby's plates.

The night was ending and damn near everyone in attendance was either drunk, buzzing or feeling some type of way even my damn parents. It wasn't a shock to see either of them in this state because my parents were both heavy drinkers, but it wasn't anything that caused a problem for us. The DJ was still spinning on the ones and twos while everyone was up dancing, enjoying each other's company along with enjoying their moods. Gingers ass was in the corner fucking it up in her own zone. She had been dancing all night. I'm surprised she hadn't passed out by now from the heat and drinks combination while dancing. I loved the fact that the functions at my parents' house were always so cordial and drama free. I think that's because muthafuckas knew my parents would not tolerate that shit and had no problem kicking your ass then putting you out with the help of my brother and me. I witnessed Erin and Dame conversing a lot throughout the day and were now sitting to the side flirting all up in each other's faces. Netia was drunk and I could see it in her eyes. She was two second away from heading inside the house and up to my room to call it a night. My plan was originally to leave my party and stay with Coby for the night but had early morning practice so it would defeat the purpose of me staying with him.

"Ohhhhhhhh shit right there, keep hitting that shit! Don't stop!" I was trying my hardest to whisper and keep my volume down but I'm not sure how successful I was with that shit the way Dupree was continuously hitting my g spot. With every thrust I could feel him taking over my warm and gushy center. "Damn Renee I love this shit! This pussy stay wet for your nigga don't it? Stop trying to fuck me back and lay you ass still before I bust!" Dupree was holding my neck like he was choking me, and that shit turned me on even more, I couldn't help but meet every thrust of his with one of my own. There's something about aggression and manhandling while fucking that would turn me on to the max. Dupree started rubbing his thumb in a circular motion on my pearl causing my legs to jerk. The sensation was slowly taking over my body and I just wanted him to make me feel the ecstasy that I had become oh so familiar with whenever we fucked. "Shit Nae put them legs over my shoulders I can't hold this shit much longer and I need to make sure I'm all the way in this pussy" "Yess, baby" I seductively moaned, after placing my legs on his shoulders like I was instructed I started bucking my hips forward to fuck him back while using his shoulder for my support going again what he had just told me about fucking him back. My entire body was lifted off the bed except my shoulders and head. Dupree started thrusting faster, harder, and deeper all while moving his thumb fast and applying more pressure to my pearl. "Yess yess, fuck! Shit! I'm cumming baby! I'm cumming!" I couldn't hold out any longer. My juices were now coating his dick and seeping down the crack of my ass. I'm no squirter but as much as I exploded you wouldn't know the difference. I felt Dupree's dick begin to jump and could tell from his pace that he was about to let lose as well. "Damn this pussy good as fuck Nae! Shiiiiiiiitttttt" Just like that he pulled out and let all of his semen escape the tip of his dick and squirt down my stomach. Since I was lying in a slanted position I could feel his nut creeping up my stomach towards my breast so I quickly dropped my legs and headed to the corner of my room to grab a towel to wipe myself off before heading out to the bathroom to freshen up and return to the party before someone noticed we were both gone.

Rushing to the bathroom I once shared with my sister at my parents' home I needed to quickly rinse off the semen that we both left as evidence on my body after our quick fuck session. Glancing in the mirror I had to look myself over to ensure I was still looking just as flawless as I did prior to sneaking away from the party. My slim fitting red Forever XX1 knee length dress was fitting every curve my body had to offer. The way my 34 "b" cup sat up without the help of a bra was amazing, my hips and ass were always decent sized but with the help of my recent pregnancy they were banging even more, I was thankful that my baby bump disappeared right after my labor and leaving me with a flat stomach as if I hadn't eve carried a child full term. Applying a thin coat of CYBER by MAC to my full plump lips and fingering my long jet-black straight hair you could never tell I was just given one of the best orgasms a woman could ask for. I couldn't help but admire my appearance in the mirror; my high cheek bones thanks to my momma, straight teeth, beautiful skin, and awesome attire was only showing how good I felt on the outside to match how I felt in the inside. I was now ready to go and finish celebrating with the rest of my family and enjoy the remainder of my evening.

My phone kept going off but after the party last night I couldn't even pull myself to wake up. The party lasted until well after one o'clock in the morning and if it wasn't for my parents both being dead tired, I'm sure it would've continued all night long. My daughter Sanai was with her father Mark and I'm sure he was the asshole who continued to blow my phone up in hopes of dropping her back off at home earlier than we originally agreed. Instead of answering the phone I simply silenced my ringtone and Laid my head back down in hopes of getting a few more hours of sleep.

BANG BANG BANG BANG

"What the fuck? Who is it" I had practically broken my neck hopping out the bed and running down the stairs of my townhome to open the door. Whoever was at the door scared me out of my sleep in the most unpleasant manner I was going to be sure to let them know by the attitude I was giving. "It's Mark! Open this damn door Nae". I snatched my front door open with the worst attitude I could possibly give him. If looks could kill his ass would've dropped right there in my doorway dropping my daughter who was in her car seat he held in hand. "Why you looking all mad and shit like I did something wrong? I was worried something may have been wrong. You never ignore all of my calls especially if I have Sanai. I been calling your ass all morning to only have my calls ignored like I don't have OUR daughter. What if it was an emergency your stupid ass couldn't been pick up the damn phone. Your ass must have had company over her or something and was scared the nigga was going to get mad at you. You could've..." I cut his ass off before he could go any fucking further. "Mark first and foremost I was sleep and we originally agreed you would keep Sanai until later this evening around 7 or 7:30 so there was no point in you blowing my phone up anytime this morning. Secondly, I know OUR daughter is just fine over your mother's house, so I was sleeping peacefully until you came over here beating on my fucking door like the damn police searching for Americas most wanted or some shit. You knew my sister's party was last night so you should've known I would have loved to sleep in for once". I grabbed Sanai's car seat from him and took it over to the couch and began to unsnap her and remove her from the seat. Mark had some fucking never coming over here because I wasn't answering his calls, he thought he was slick the only reason he brought Sanai home so early and popped up was to see if I had someone over. Unlike his stupid ass I wouldn't be stupid enough to get caught up by doing the obvious.

Mark walked further into my home and he shut and locked the front door as if I welcomed his ass inside to chill for a second when I didn't. Mark and I once shared my townhome before we separated for the last time not long ago. We had been on and off again boyfriend and girlfriend for the past four years and honestly our relationship had taken its course but like all women I was still holding on hoping things would go back to the way they used to be. I probably would've still been trying to work shit out between us two if I wouldn't have caught him red handed fucking some girl outside of the Club in the backseat of his Royal Blue Infinity Truck. There was no way I planned on taking him back after seeing things with my own eye, I mean I always assumed he would cheat a time or two over the year based on his own careless decisions and slip up but I never had any solid proof until that night. Mark couldn't believe I was completely done with his sorry ass until he tried to come home the following morning and my locks were changed and all of his clothes were neatly packed in boxes waiting for his arrival on the porch. I didn't feel there was any need for us to talk about what happened the night before what was done was done and there was no taking back what I witnessed. Although I wanted to work it out for the sake of our daughter but if I accepted that type of disrespect it would only get worse and I don't know how I would've reacted to something like that happening on the regular.

Holding Sanai, little beautiful self-admiring her in her sleep was something I did so often. My baby was absolutely beautiful. She would remind you of one of those beautiful chocolate babies you see in the magazines. Sanai had the perfect chocolate skin complexion with a head full of jet black curly hair, big bright brown eyes, the fattest cheeks you couldn't help but kiss or rub every time you came in contact with her, she had the cutest little puckered up lips, and a round button nose. Admiring Sanai's beauty, it caused me to totally forget Mark had walked upstairs and had yet to come back down, I knew he was only snooping around looking for hints of a man being in my home but he was taking too long to come back down. I laid my baby in her pack and play in the corner of the Livingroom and decided to head upstairs to help Mark's slick ass find his way right back downstairs and out of my home. Rather he was the father of my daughter and ex-boyfriend. It was no longer his place or position to check shit about how I was living my life as long as no harm was brought to his daughter in the process. After checking Sanai's room, our bathroom, I walked into my bedroom and spotted Mark stretched across my King-size Canopy bed with his shoes off and eyes closed as if he had fallen asleep right there. This nigga must have forgot he was put out and that was no longer OUR bed but MY bed and there was no way I was going to allow his ass to sleep there peacefully considering he had just ruined my peaceful sleep with popping up and pulling the I was worried card. "Mark get your ass up and out of my bed nigga" I started pulling at his right arm trying to wake him up. "Renee stop playing, just lay back down and finish getting your rest. I'm tired. I had a long night I'm tired." He stated groggily and calm like he thought I would seriously consider laying back down with him and pretending that we were some happy ass couple. Mark had another thing coming if he thought he was about to just lay there in my bed and ignore the fact I wanted him gone. So, I pulled Mark by his arm again only this time pulling it hard as I possibly could. I was pulling his arm like I wanted to yank his arm out of the socket while yelling for him to get the fuck out my bed and go back home to his momma house because he no longer lived here. Before I could yank again Mark instantly reached over with his left arm and landed the hardest smack to the right side of my face causing me to stumble back a little. I reached up and grabbed my face. I was in shock that he just reacted the way he did. Mark wasn't your average size nigga, so the smack felt more like a fucking punch. As bad as I wanted to defend myself, I knew there would be no competition between the two of us. I only stood 5'7, weighing 145-pound soaking wet compared to him standing 6 feet plus and weighing well over two hundred and fifty pounds of solid muscle. "Renee I'm so sick of you acting like I'm your fucking bitch or some shit I told you to leave me alone, damn not look what the fuck you made me do?" He was now sitting up on the edge of my bed and putting his shoes on his feet like what he had just done was normal or acceptable. I couldn't even move I was still in shock that Mark would really smack me in my face while our daughter was downstairs and because I was only trying to get him out of my bed and home. Mark had hit me before on a few different occasions over the years, but it was before I became pregnant with my daughter, he promised he would never hit me again the last time. My daughter is eight months, so it had been well over a year since he put hands on me, so I actually believed him.

Mark walked right past me without ever looking at me and headed downstairs. I hoped he was really leaving this time, as bad as I wanted to lay across my bed and cry from the physical and mental pain, I refused to shed another tear over Mark after that night I caught him cheating. I wouldn't give him the satisfaction of ever hurting me again. I promise if it's the last thing I do I'm going to get all of my pay back no matter how long it takes me to do it. Mark will feel every ounce of pain he ever caused me times ten. I heard my front door slam and Marks tires screeching out of my drive so I knew he was gone, he better not have scared my daughter from her nap with his stupidity or It would only speed the process with me getting back at his sorry ass. Running down the stairs to my living room to check on Sanai I was happy she was still sleeping peacefully as if nothing had ever just happened. After ensuring my baby was ok and grabbing the baby monitor to take along with me upstairs, I headed to take a shower and get my day started.

Standing in the shower allowing the water to run through my hair, the thought of Mark's actions, fidelity, lies, and broken promises only pushed my thoughts to Dupree and how sincere he had been to me over the years. Dupree and I had been messing around only for a year and a half, but we had always crushed on each other. I tried to keep him in the friend zone because of his relationship with my brother, but you can't help who your heart desires nor who wants you in return. Shit Dupree should've been considered a brother to me as well, but I could never look at him in that way even after being around him for damn near my entire life. Dupree and my brother had been friends since grade school along with their other friend Dame, so he was considered to be family to everyone else but me. Dupree has been in my corner even more since I got pregnant and he even sneaks' money in my purse or pockets whenever we are around each other. He knows that I work to provide for me and my child and can depend on my parents if shit ever gets bad but knowing my attitude along with who I am won't allow me to accept anything from others he sneaks to provides for me as well Sanai. Instead of returning the money I always put it into a separate account that I opened for Sanai before she was born. Around the time I conceived my daughter I had sex with Dupree on a drunk night at one of my parent's famous parties. It was the first time I had ever slept with Dupree and I was so fucked up I didn't even protest that he should have worn a condom, but I came home and fucked Mark the next morning so I never thought about the fact that Sanai could have possibly been Dupree's. My daughter looked nothing like Mark and only had few features that belong to me, so I just assumed it was because she was so young. I hope as she gets a little older her looks become more defined because as of right now, I have no clue who my baby looks like including myself. I don't know how I would even bring the subject up to my family or even Lee and she's not only my little sister but best friend. Mark has been her father since day one and like they say if it's not broke don't fix it. Mark may be a sorry ass boyfriend, but he is in fact a pretty good father. Mark signed her birth certificate and he had been her father all this time so until proven differently I'm just going to leave well enough alone.

I grabbed a pair of Miss Me jeans from my closest and peach colored Affliction shirt to match a pair of flat peach colored sandals I had purchased months ago but never worn. I'm going for a dress down yet still cute type of day. I didn't feel like dressing in my normal skirt, dress, or girly attire but that still didn't mean I would be ok with looking a mess. I take pride in my appearance and I wouldn't be caught dead looking a mess no matter how I was feeling at the moment. After applying some Crème of Nature Twirling Custard to my naturally curly from washing my hair in the shower, I placed a cute Peach artificial flower by my ear to give my afro so cuteness. Puckering up with my lips with my Nude MAC lipstick, my look for the day was now completed. Thank God for my brown skin complexion there was no bruising left from the smack Mark had landed on my face one an hour prior or I would've had to rush and go buy some makeup to cover that shit so no one noticed it. I'm happy Mark had at least taken the time out and gotten Sanai dressed for the day before bringing her home so that was one less worry, I only needed to change her diaper and repack her back for items we might need while out being out and about today. Our first stop would be my parents' house to see if they needed any help with cleaning up after last night.

My parents lived on the opposite side of town, so it took me about twenty-five minutes to arrive at their house. Plus, it was Saturday so there wasn't any type of traffic to hold me up from coasting to their side of town. Pulling up in the driveway I noticed My brothers all White 2014 Dodge Charger I prepared to be face to face with Dupree which put a smile on my face. I climbed out of my Altima and headed to the opposite side of the car to grab Sanai and her bag, but I could see Lee running towards my car with her arms out. "Hey Renee! Give me my Baby Baby!" The love and attention that Lee showed my daughter you would've thought it was her damn baby that I carried and housed for her. Lee would take Sanai any chance she got the opportunity to. I even let Lee name her when she was born because she was so in Love with Sanai before she even came into this world. My sister didn't miss a beat my entire pregnancy; she was at every appointment along with me and even stayed with me when I was discharged from the hospital to help me out for the first week. My little sister was my best friend although we4 have separate lives and we mind our own business. I couldn't have asked for a great sister. When I do decide to tell my secret about the possibility of Sanai's father Lee would be the first for me to tell just because of all the people I knew she wouldn't pass judgement on me and have my back no matter who my baby daddy may be.

Walking into the house you couldn't tell that there was a huge party just the night before. The house was back to normal just like it appeared any other day. My dad was sitting in his recliner watching Law and Order drinking his Budweiser like every Saturday. I thought by it being still so early in the day they would still be recuperating from last night shit it was only 1 o'clock in the afternoon. "hey daddy!" "Hey Hunny" He replied to my greeting and I kissed him on the cheek from behind before heading to the kitchen to see my mother. Of course, my mother was in here preparing food as always like she hadn't cooked enough for the rest of the month with the food she prepared yesterday but to my surprise there weren't any leftovers. "Momma! Your favorite has arrived!" I said jokingly, I always claimed to be my mother's favorite child even though she never showed any difference in any of us, she always just agreed with me whenever my siblings weren't around. "Well hello there my favorite child! How are you today! And where is my grandbaby?" "I'm doing good, still sleepy as heck from yesterday! I planned to sleep in today but of course Mark had other plans and dropped Sanai off to me at eleven thirty when our original plan was for him to bring her to me tonight by seven thirty. Sanai is somewhere around here with Lee." I climbed on one of the bar stools and started looking through my phone like I always do when I sit in the kitchen and admire my mother thrown down on whatever it is she prepares. "Marks ass is something else. He still has a lot of maturing to do and hopefully he does it soon for the sake of my grandbaby if he's going to continue to be in yawl's life." My mother turned around and looked at me out of the corner of her eye like she was insinuating something. I brushed it off and went back to checking my missed calls and text messages from this morning while my phone was on silent. "I just wish he would get the point. I'm so sick of him and wish he would just leave me alone forever! Even if he was to mature overnight, I still don't believe that nigga will get the point." I stated. My mother knows all about Mark's lies and cheating but I never told her about him being domestic with me. My mother was very close to my sister and I and has always been so I feel comfortable talking to her about any and everything, but I knew that would only be signing Mark's death certificate if I confessed to him hitting me. "Baby one thing I will tell you that I've learned over the years when a woman is fed up there is no maturing that will be enough when it comes to a man! Mark will come around to his senses but trust me when I tell you it will be too late it will be far too late for you to even care." I noticed I had an unread text message from Dupree when I was getting ready to respond to my mother's last comment. "Mommy you're so right and I know you are because whenever you give us advice or insight, they are always dead on." I opened the message that I missed from Dupree and a smile spread across my face on accident.

Dupree: Good morning beautiful! I know you're still asleep but call me when you wake up so we can do breakfast or something.

Dupree: Damn you still sleep? Just forget it a nigga will starve waiting on your sleeping beauty ass. LOL

Dupree and I had just started back messing around after I broke off things with Mark. After our first encounter I avoided him and ignored any text or call from him because I was with Mark and felt like shit for even having sex with him. Even though the night I gave in and had sex with Dupree me and Mark were technically broken up we were still living together. The following morning, I went home and made up to Mark as if I was the reason we were fighting to begin with out of guilt. "Child what you over there doing in that phone that got your face all lite up and glowing?" My mother asked with a slight smile on her face. She always paid attention to our moods and our lives so she hardly ever missed a beep. "Nothing reading these text moms, with your nosey self" I stated jokily and laughed before replying to the text Dupree sent me earlier.

Me: Sorry I silenced my phone so I could sleep in but that didn't work. Where are you at?

Dupree: At your parents' house with Kris. Where you at?

Me: In the kitchen talking to my mom. I'll be out there in a minute.

Dupree: Ok beautiful see you in a second.

I placed my phone on the counter then went to the refrigerator to grab me a bottle of water before going to find Lee and my baby. My parents' house was still considered home no matter how long ago I moved out, they never changed my old room. It was still mine and even had a few new additions to it for Sanai although she had her own area in their room for the nights they would keep her. I could hear Lee in her room singing Yo Gabba Gabba "Party in my tummy" like it was the new hit single for the summer, so I knew Sanai was awake and playing with her aunty. Opening the door my sister was in full blown concert mood standing up dancing in front of my baby who was sitting up in the middle of Lee's bed smiling and giggling at her crazy Aunt. "Lee you are a mess! Yawl two crack me up!" I stated while admiring the two of them with a smile on my face. "Get out Nae you're interrupting us" Lee instructed me because my daughter's attention was broken by my presence in the room. I simply waved her off and headed right back down the stairs to grab my phone before going out back to see what was up with my brother and say hello to Dupree in person.

"What's up Kris! Hey Dame, Hey Dupree! What yawl foo's out here doing?" I greeted all three of them before sliding the patio door back closed behind me. All three of them were chilling on the patio smoking a blunt and enjoying this August weather. "What's up Nae" Dame and Dupree both said in unison. Dupree looked over at me and I could see the lust in his eyes. I just hoped it wasn't as evident to everyone else as it was to me. I licked my lips and smiled before Kris spoke and got my attention back. "What's up sis? Shit chilling out! When you get here?" Kris asked "Not long I just got here about fifteen minutes ago, but shit I'm going back in the house I'm not about to be out here with yawl catching contact from that shit" I started laughing and turned to head back into the house as they all laughed at me. Whatever they were smoking on was strong as hell and the smoke was filling my nostril by the second. I wasn't perfect nor a goody two shoes but Couldn't handle weed, I'd rather have a drink or pop a pill occasionally and that was rare.

I decided to head back to the kitchen to accompany my mother since everyone else was in their own zones and she was the only person who I wouldn't be interrupting by my presence. "Renee grab me some plates from the cabinet and put them over there" She said pointing to the counter where I was just sitting. My mother believed that a hot meal was the only way to do things no matter how many times of day or week you had to cook, it was rare she would prefer to go out to eat instead of cooking at home. "Is the food done already mommy?" "Yep it sure is I'm bout to load this dishwasher and you can go ahead and make your plate. Your dad said he isn't ready to eat so I'm about to join him and catch up on this Law and Order" "You would think yawl would've watch every episode by now as much as you two watch that show" "Shit we probably have but don't know until we already good and into it." My phone started vibrating on the counter notifying me of a text message. Then went off again before I could get over to it. When I picked it up, seeing Mark's name caused a change in my entire mood. What the fuck could he possibly want after the bullshit he pulled this morning? Then there was a text message from Dupree which helped to bring the smile back to my face.

Mark: I'm sorry for the way I responded this morning Renee, I just have a lot going on and it's starting to take a toll on me being away from you and our daughter on a daily basis. I'm not used to this much distance and space between us for this long. Baby I'm sorry and I want things to work between us, I'm willing to do whatever it takes to make things right and fix all my wrong doings. Renee you don't know how much you two mean to me! Just let me know when you are free and back at home so I can stop by and I have something I would like to give you. I know you two are out and about because I tried to stop by the apartment, and I didn't see your car. I Love you baby!

Instead of replying I simply exit out of the message and went to read what Dupree had sent me.

Dupree: You look even more beautiful with your hair like that Nae! You got my man's ready to break free.

Me: Thank you baby! Oh, is he? Well may be able to fix that in just a few but the food is ready if yawl hungry.

Dupree: Ok we bout to head in there anyways. Stop teasing a nigga and licking them lips the way you do, and I wouldn't be out here on rock hard. LOL

Me: I'm sorry baby I can't help how my body responds when I see something that I know is oh so tasty.

Texting Dupree and thinking of the things that man does to my body cause a tingling sensation between my legs. I put my phone in my back pocket and Started making my plate before my brother and them came in with the munchies and took over the entire kitchen. Baked smothered pork chops with gravy, broccoli with cheese, home-made mash potatoes and a dinner roll was not on your average lunch menu, but it was what my mom had in mind for our lunch. I blame my mom for all the hips and ass me and Lee have thanks to all these hefty meals. It seemed like we never could pick up any weight in the stomach again but all our weight went straight to our ass and hips with every meal. No sooner than I sat down on the bar stool with my plate and bowed my head to say grace my brother, Dame, and Dupree were walking into the kitchen from out back and Lee was heading into the kitchen from the opposite direction. The aroma of food took over the kitchen so the stitch of weed from their smoke session didn't seem as strong as it was when I was just outside with them moments ago. "Damn Nae slow down you couldn't even wait on us to start eating, shit you could've at least made my plate" Kris said jokily. Kris always felt like he was supposed to eat right after my dad since he was "The man" around here as well. My mother spoiled not only my father but my brother as well, so he felt like he deserved King treatment from any and every female he came in contact with. I found it funny at times, but he had me fucked up if he thought I was about to make his plate and wait on his ass when he was totally capable of doing it his damn self. "Nigga I don't know who you thought you were coming in here making demands and request, I'm not your momma and I'm not you bitch so you better get to making your own damn plate if you know what's best." We all started laughing. Lee made her plate and sat next to me on a bar stool. For some reason we always chose to eat at the counter instead of the table if we were eating as a family at the table.

"Renee! I think Mark is pulling up" My mother called out from the Living Room

"What did you say mom?" I wanted to make sure I heard her right! I know this nigga didn't feel the need to pop up at my parents' house after I chose not to respond to any of his text or calls. With the shit he pulled this morning I had every right to ignore him, I don't know what part of us being over didn't Mark understand.

"Yep it sure it, Mark just pulled up! Better go and see what he wants because it doesn't seem like he's getting out of that car" As soon as those words left my mother's lips, I could feel Dupree's stares burning a hole in the side of my face. I chose to ignore the feeling of his eyes watching me and go see what Mark could possibly want. Hopping off the bar stool and placing my napkin on the counter, I grabbed my phone before heading out the front door.

Mark was sitting in his front seat with his attention on his phone, he was so into whatever it was on his phone he hadn't realized me walking towards his car until I was pulling at the passenger side door handle. My guess is I startled him because he jumped before hitting the unlock button to allow me access to his car. I climbed into the front seat and made a point to slam his car door a little harder than usual so he could hint at the attitude I still had from earlier.

"Damn Nae Why you have to shut the door so hard?" Mark said in a joking manner with an attempt to lighten my mood.

"What's up Mark?" There was no need for me to beat around the bush. I was ready to know what was so important he felt the need to show up looking for me even after I didn't return his text. The sooner he got what he needed to say off his chest the sooner I could get back into the house.

"Nae first I wanted to start by telling you again that I'm sorry for the way I acted this morning. Secondly, I hate how things are going between us. I just want things to go back to the way they were. I can't stand this wedge between us and I can't stand the thought of you moving on to be with the next nigga and living happily ever after with my daughter. Just let me know how I can fix this shit between us!" He sounded so sincere but so did he every other time we broke up just to make right back up when I fell for his bullshit excuses and apologies. Mark's phone started ringing as soon as he was finished speaking and I glanced over to see if I could catch a sneak peek at who was calling, but I failed at my attempt to be nosey. He quickly pressed the red button on his screen ignoring the caller as if what we were talking about was that important.

"Listen Mark! Honestly, there isn't anything we can do to fix this! Our relationship has run its course. We were over way before we were really over. I don't want to work on fixing us because I don't feel that it was us who ruined US, it was you." I didn't feel the need to lie or pretend we could work it out because I really wanted and needed for him to understand that I was done trying.

"What the fuck do you mean we are over. Renee we will never be over you are the mother of my child and I'm not accepting the fact that your too pissed off at me right now to fix it!" Mark was now practically yelling at me and his teeth were clenched with every word that he spoke.

"Look Mark I don't want to go through this right now! But like I said I'm done, and I don't want to work this out" I pointed to the both of us to signal me and him is what I was referring to. I reached for the handle to the door so I could get out the truck and was stopped by Mark yanking my left arm back with the tightest grip possible. "Mark please let go of my arm. I'm not trying to go there with you" My phone rang, and it was Dupree calling. He must have been either watching out the window or felt disrespected that I was outside with Mark for so long. As of lately he was starting to become annoyed with Mark's presence and he had no problem letting me know. "Hello" I greeted Dupree when I answered the phone with a dry tone. "You coo out there?" Dupree asked. "Yeah, here I come." I answered the best I could without letting Mark know exactly who I was on the phone with inside of the house and ended the call.

"Renee, I love you and I'm not letting you go that easy! I'll let you get back to whatever you were doing but I can promise you this isn't the end of this conversation nor US!" Mark stated before letting loose of the grip he had on my arm.

Getting out of the truck and slamming his door once again I headed back to my mother's house and I hadn't noticed that Dupree was sitting on the front porch by himself. I could only hope he wasn't sitting here the entire time. Dupree looked up at me and I could see the anger in his eyes.

3

ERIN

his day couldn't go by any fucking slower, I don't know who the fuck told me to pick up work on my day off anyhow. I guess this is the price I have to pay in order to live comfortably. Don't get me wrong I like my job. It's pretty laid back, pays well, and has great benefits for a nineteen-year-old with no children. The people at my job are pretty cool too. We have people ranging from all ages and backgrounds. I would have never imagined working for a call center let alone the Chase bank call center would be so laid back. The only problem I have is the attire we have to wear. I mean don't get me wrong I like to dress up when I feel like it but no every fucking day.

Tonight, I had plans on meeting up with Dame to have a few drinks and maybe catch a movie. Walking to my car I decided to send my girls a message. We had a group chat we were all in so whenever we didn't feel like calling each other on three way we could send a simple message and it would reach all of us.

Me: hey ladies! Guess who's off work? I'm hungry as hell and need to go grab something to wear from the mall who's down to ride?

Lee: Hey boo! I'm hungry too but I'm with Coby at the moment wish you would've told me earlier.

Netia: hey yawl! Shit I'm down come get me, my mom getting on my fucking nerves any damn way. LOL

Me: I just decided to go sorry boo but spend time with you man shit you the one bout to move far the fuck away: (and Tia I'm on my way bitch be ready.

Lee: Don't say it like that: (you're making me feel bad!

Netia: Bitch I been dressed and ready to leave this house since I woke up call me when you're outside, you know what better, yet I'll be on the fucking porch waiting. LOL

I closed out of our group text and started my car and headed to Natia's house to pick her up. Just thinking about Lee moving away to college made me think of all the shit I was going to miss, I mean it's not like I can't call her or go visit but she wouldn't be up the street she would be hours away. I'm happy that she decided to go to college, but I just wish she would have picked a closer school. I graduated last year and instead of going off to college I chose to go straight to work, there was no way I was about to put myself in thousands of dollars into debt only to land a job that wouldn't be able to pay off the loans even if I tried, but Lee was bless to get a full ride so more power to her. I'm glad she's spending time with Coby before she leaves though. Coby is a great guy and he treats Lee like gold, when we first met Coby and his boys over a year ago, I would have never thought him, and Lee would have talked let alone be together this long and happy. My girl loves her some Coby and he loves him some Lee. They have the cutest relationship. I can only hope that when I get into a serious relationship that it will be half as good as the one my girl has with Coby. Me and Netia just can't seem to luck up just yet on a good nigga. Netia's ass I think has given up all hope on finding her a nigga, sometimes I think the bitch be eating pussy on the low but just doesn't want us to find out. Whenever a nigga approaches her, she turns his ass down at hello, but always want to suggest we take our ass to the strip club to see some damn half naked bitches shaking their pussy in our faces.

Netia's ass was serious when she said she would be waiting for me on the porch, I had to laugh when I spotted her silly looking ass sitting on the porch with her head resting on her arm pouting like a little ass kid. I swear when she saw my car pull into the driveway her face lit up and she damn near hopped from the top step to the bottom in such a rush to get to my car.

"Damn bitch too you long enough!" Netia got in the car talking cash shit as always.

"Shut up bitch, I only work all the way in Polaris and your ass lives clear across the fucking country. Besides there was construction on the freeway so you know how that shit be when its only one fucking lane open for traffic." Netia didn't respond; she only hooked her IPhone up to the AUX cord to my radio and scrolled through her playlist on her phone stopping at Gucci. I swear for her to be the most quiet girl she loves her some damn trap music, but I wasn't complaining because I fucked with Gucci the long way regardless of how old he was to everyone else.

They ain't got nothin' on ya.

They ain't got nothin' on ya (They ain't got nothin' on ya)

I swear them hoes, they ain't got nothin' on ya

That nigga broke, he ain't got nothin' for ya

Natia and I both reached to turn the volume up and laughed. This was our shit and every time we heard it no matter where the location, we were sure enough ready to have a full blown twerk session. I swear this is how me and my bitches felt whenever we were out at the club or event when it came to the other females. When it came to shutting shit down, we had no completion, well none our age at least. Not trying to boost me and my friend up but we were all the true definition of BAD. I would consider myself to be a 15 on a scale from 1 to 10. Although I'm the tallest out the crew it wasn't like I was some Jolly Green Giant or some shit. I stood about 5'7, 5'8 depending if I had on my shoes or not. Weighing 190 but not a roll of fat in sight, I've been a dancer my entire life from little league cheerleading to drill team in high school, so my body was in good shape. Thanks to great genes I was blessed with hips, thighs, and the ass of a video vixen. Unfortunately, that's where all my weight went to because I was definitely rocking a 36 "A" cup with the flattest stomach. I rocked my hair in a short bob cut most of the time and I switch up the color damn near on a monthly basis. Although my real hair is cut in a bob as well, I like to rock the quick weaves it's so much easier to deal with and I can change colors whenever without worrying about my shit falling out shortly after. I'm on the lighter side but I like to refer to my skin complexion as more of a peanut butter brown, dark brown slanted eyes, I have a set of full plum lips and a dimple in the middle of my chin that I got from my mother.

When we pulled up to Easton Mall there wasn't a parking spot in sight. For it to be the middle of the day you would think that people would have their asses at work instead of the mall. I mean it was a Wednesday but damn. Times like this I wish I had a handicap stick so I could just pull up and jump out and be on my fucking way. The worst part of shopping is always finding a good parking spot and carrying in the bags after the trip. I finally found a parking spot and headed into the mall towards ALDO first. When it comes to shopping, I always like to find the shoes I would be wearing first then work my way up. As soon as we stepped foot in the mall, I'll be damn if we didn't run smack dead into Mark and some bitch. The girl looks like she was younger than Renee and Renee had a baby face, but she had on so much fucking makeup you would've thought she was headed to the damn circus. Mark is Lee's older sister Renee's baby dad and long-time boyfriend. This nigga was bold to be flaunting round town with a bitch on his arm when I'm sure Renee was at work with her old faithful ass. That nigga has always been a dog we had spotted him on numerous occasions doing so foul shit but never at the mall in the middle of the damn day for any and everybody to see the shit. Witnessing the embarrassment Renee had to deal with because of his cheating ways were all reasons I didn't mind being single. I'm the type of bitch that would run up on both of them and fuck some shit up without a second thought and worry about the consequences later.

"Bitch ain't that Marks ass right there?" Netia asked in a whispering tone.

"Sure, the fuck is snap a picture and send it to group text I'm bout to call Lee and tell her this shit." Call it childish shit call it what you want but that nigga was busted once again and there would be no denying it if we had proof. As soon as Netia snapped the picture Mark made eye contact with us and turned the other way with the thang he had attached to his arm. He saw us just like we had seen him, but he wanted to pretend he didn't because he knew my slick ass mouth would say something to the both of them with no hesitation.

Lee answered on the third ring. "Oh, hell no is that Marks ass with some clown looking broad on his arm?" Lee questioned. She must have had her phone in hand because she got that picture message quick as fuck.

"Hell, yeah it is, then after Netia snapped the picture the nigga looked at us and had the nerve to turn and walk the opposite direction like he didn't see us eyeing them both. He better be happy I'm on a mission to grab my outfit and get the fuck out the packed as mall or Would've hauled ass over there and embarrassed him and the silly looking hoe he with." Lee started laughing, she knew I was dead as serious. "Bitch you laughing and I'm serious as hell" I said in a more serious tone. Only causing Lee to laugh at me even harder.

"Oh, bitch I know you are that's what makes it so funny. I can just picture your ass walking over to them and being funny. Damn I wish I was there that nigga may have taken off running in the opposite direction and left his clown of a hoe standing there all by her damn self." Lee said with her tone now matching my seriousness.

"It would've been all bad for his ass if you were here with us. But get back to your boo, we bout to walk into ALDO and I'm sure I'm going to lose service, so I'll hit you up a little later. Bye boo"

"Bye, don't yawl get into no shit without me"

"Bye girl we ain't" I said before ending our call. There was no way I was getting into no shit because I had plans for later tonight. This would be the first time I chilled with Dame and it wouldn't be at one of the Lees parent's parties.

"I don't know what Renee seeing in that dog ass nigga I would've been fuck around and left his ass by now after this long and still not getting shit right. That nigga should've put on Renee's finger by now instead of walking around arm and arm with the next bitch." Netia said with a disgusted look on her face and I could completely under-stand what she meant.

"Girl who you telling. But shit if Nae likes it I love it. She got to know he's still cheating and out here doing his thing like he's single or some shit. Nae may be a little on the dingy side but she far from dumb."

After three hours of walking around what felt like the whole damn Easton Mall area, I had finally found an outfit for tonight that I was pleased with. It was an all-purpose outfit, the perfect mixture or classy, cut, yet sexy all in one. Instead of going out to eat, Netia opted to grab something lite from the food court inside the mall so we ate as we walked from store to store. Five Guys was the best burger joint and it was filling enough to hold me off until later tonight when I met up with Dame. I dropped Netia off at her cousin's house on my way home and told her I would text or call her later after my date. I still had yet to tell the girls who I was going on a date with, but that could wait until after I see how our first date turned out. My girls knew I couldn't hold water so they didn't even question who because they knew by the end of the night, I would be informing them on who the mystery man was.

Dame had just called and told me he would be pulling up to my apartment in about fifteen minutes. I had just finished feathering the curls in my bob with my flat iron to give myself the finishing touches. The six-inch peep toe mustard color wedge heels I found in ALDO, straight leg skinny jeans, and Mustard colored "v" neck wrap around shirt looked amazing on my body. I even topped it off with gold accessories and gold lipstick. Just as I unplugged the flat iron my phone started vibrating on the bathroom sink and I knew it was Dame calling to let me know he was outside. Just as I expected when I looked at the screen of my phone sure enough it was him. Sliding my finger across the screen to answer his call I rushed to grab my mustard colored clutch and keys before heading out the door.

"Hey, here I come. I'm bout to lock my door and head down the stairs now." I didn't even give him the time to tell me he was outside before letting him know I was on my way to him.

"Yep" Was all he said before ending the call.

As soon as I opened the passenger side door to Dame Gray 2011 Dodge charger his cologne filled my nose, that shit was intoxicating I had to find out what the brand was. Dame, Kris, and Dupree all had 2011 Dodge Charger that they had all purchased at the same time. I don't know who them niggas thought they were, but the shit was pretty fly if you asked me.

"Well hello miss lady, you looking sexy as fuck tonight." Dame looked at me with the sexiest grin I had ever seen in my entire 19 years of living.

"Thanks sweetie, you look good too I must admit" I said trying not to show how much his comment had made me blush. That's the one thing I headed about being a lighter complexion my emotions would always show with the shades my skin would change. I could feel my cheeks turning by the second and started to get a little shy.

The movie we originally wanted to see was sold out for the night, so we ended up hitting up the Arena District to get a few drinks. The first bar we headed to Dame knew the nigga who worked at the door, so he was able to get me in without the guy ever asking for my Id. I had totally forgotten about being under 21 when he mentioned Arena District because I was so caught up on just being out on a date with him. Going to the bar was the wrong idea because it was only a quarter after twelve and I was already beyond wasted. Dame kept ordering us rounds of drink over the course of our conversation and me not wanting to appear to be a lightweight we taking the back to back with his ass. I could tell he was too feeling the effects of the 1800 we were drinking because his eyes were low. I knew his high had worn down from the blunt he smoked on the way there because Dame was a chronic smoker and we had been sitting here for well over an hour. Damn reached over and gripped my thigh and I instantly felt the rush take over my entire body. I don't know if it was the liquor or the fact that I had been lusting over this nigga for years and was finally in his presence and on an actual date with him. Dame's firm grip on my thigh had me thinking of all the other places he could grip just as tight causing me to become hornier than I had ever been.

"You ready to get outta here I'm feeling the little drinks and I need to roll up?" Dame broke me away from my wandering thoughts that I hadn't realized I drifted off into.

"Yeah that's coo, I'm buzzed my damn self." I lied a little because I was beyond buzzed, I was well over fucked up.

We were walking to Dames car and he wrapped his arm around my shoulder pulling me closer to him. The smell of his cologne mixed with those many drinks I had taken were causing my juices to fill my underwear. I was thankful for wearing a pair of dark jeans because I was sure there would've been evidence left on my pants. I don't know what Dame has in mind, but I know I'm trying to see what he had between those legs of his and I don't know if I can hold out any longer. As soon as we were seated in the car Dame wasted no time going into his arm rest and recovering his stash of weed and shell to rollup. Lighting his blunt and starting his car we were pulling off blasting Fetty Wap.

"You with me for the night or am I taking you back to your crib?" Dame asked me and of course I already had the answer to that question.

"Take me back to my house please, but I want you to stay with me." Dame smiled and gave me a slight nod while taking a hit from his blunt before reaching over and offering it to me. I reached over and grabbed it and took a few puffs before passing it back.

My foot wasn't completely in the front door before Dame was all over me. I reached back and twisted my bottom lock and kicked the front door shut. I dropped my clutch, phone and keys on the couch and led him straight to my bedroom. I was happy that I always kept my house clean and Glade Plug-ins because I would've felt like trash bringing him back to a nasty house that didn't at least smell clean. Dame was undressing as soon as we hit my bedroom. I sat on the edge of my bed and removed my wedges before standing back up to remove my pants along with my shirt. Looking up I swear Dame had grown a third leg that niggas dick was hanging damn near to his kneecap and my mouth dropped before I knew it.

"Damn ma that look on your face tells me you weren't expecting a sight like this" Dame said, giving me that same sexy grin he had been giving me all night but only this time with lustful eyes that were scanning my entire body. If I never felt so shy now, I was. But now was not the time to get shy. I had to put my big girl panties on and prepare for what was about to go down.

"Cat go your tongue Ma? Come here why you sitting over there looking all shy now?" Instead of responding I stood up and walked over to where Dame was standing.

"Damn Erin you bad as fuck fa real Ma! I mean I knew your body was cold but the clothes wasn't doing no justice for you. Then the way your ass sitting up in this thong got my dick on swole." Dame was now cupping my ass cheeks with the same strong grip he had on my thigh earlier at the bar as I wrapped my arms around his neck and started kissing on the nape of his neck. I didn't know how he would respond if I started sucking on his neck but the way he was making my body feel in his embrace I had to at least get a taste of him. I started licking his neck followed by kisses when I felt his hand ripping my thong off of me, I was caught a little off guard yet turned on by his aggression. Dame reached for my center and I felt his fingers begin to explore my jewels. Just his touch caused me to let out a slight moan. He was caressing my clit and I felt my legs begin to get weak. The more he massaged the wetter I became. Dame pushed me back against the wall and dropped down in front of me. I grabbed my leg and placed my foot on his shoulder. He started licking the lips of my pussy and kissing them as if they were the lips on my face. That shit turned me on so fucking much. Using his two fingers to spread my lips a little wider I felt his warm tongue begin to flicker over my clit and I could no longer hold in the moans that were trying to escape my mouth. As his tongue continued to flicker over my clit, I felt him insert two fingers inside of me and he instantly connected to my G spot. Dame started fingering my pussy faster and blew on my clit lightly and my legs began to tremble. I started moaning louder and cum began to ooze from my body as if he had just caused an eruption of fluids that had never been released. He stood to his feet and walked over to the bed and I followed him. I laid down on the bed and spread my legs to give him a full view of my pussy. I began to play with my clit and he quickly removed my hand and started slapping the tip of his dick on my sensitive clit giving me the urge to cum again. Dame pushed my legs back and inserted his entire dick inside of me in one swift motion. I tensed up because of the pain but I wouldn't allow him to know that it was hurting so bad. I had never had a dick this big shit I had only fuck two men ever and neither of the combined were the size of Dame. I guess that what you get when you go from fucking with boys to men. I held my hands up and tried to push Dame back some so I could get a little more comfortable with his size before he started pumping inside of me but he only swatted my hands down and pushed further inside of me. I swear his dick was touching my heart.

"Nah ma don't run from it. I'm bout to give your young ass some of this grown man dick. This pussy tight as fuck I know after this you ain't going want to ever fuck another.IS you ready Ma?"

"yes Dame, yes I'm ready" I responded

"Nah ma when I'm in this pussy you refer to me as daddy. You hear me?" Dame started fucking me and I swear he was knowing every vital organ out of place, but the pain was a good pain. The feeling was indescribable. He was right, it was something I had never felt before and I was loving every minute of it.

"yes...yess daddy! Yess it feels soo good! It feels so good. Don't stop." The more I moaned the harder he went, and I felt my cum leaking out of me I was cumming back to back and it didn't seem like I could stop it. My entire body was shaking, and I just wanted to scream.

"Damn Erin this pussy is fire, this shit just keeps getting wetter and wetter for me! You like this shit? Na don't even answer me that pussy talking for you. Don't worry I like this phat ass pussy too. This shit...ohhh damn this shit goin make a nigga lock you down fa real ma." Dame just didn't know but from the moment he ate my pussy it was locked down. He was giving me orgasms I had never experienced, and I had no plans on ever sharing it again with another young nigga as he called them.

"Oh, shit daddy I'm cumming don't stop. Fuck me! Yess fuck me daddy!" I've never been a real loud moaner, but this nigga was taking me through it with the dick he was delivering.

"Shit Ma! I'm bout to nut where you want me to put it?" Dame asked throwing me off, but I was so into it I just responded with the first thing that came to mind.

"Put it in my mouth daddy!" And Dame pulled out of me so fast I thought I was going to choke at the speed he shoved his big as dick in my throat. I was still lying flat on the bed and he was now fucking my face and his nut was draining down my throat. I started sucking and squeezing his dick with my hand trying to make sure I got every ounce. This was the first time I had ever let a nigga nut in my mouth let alone swallow the shit. Dame's nut didn't taste too bad after all and the way he was moaning encouraged me even more.

"Erin what you trying to do to a nigga suck my soul out?" Damn asked laughing as he fell over on his back in my bed. I playfully slapped his chest and got up to wash my face off. By the time I washed off and brushed my teeth Dame was fast asleep on my bed with only his boxers and socks. Dame was even sexy when he slept. He was a shade lighter than and to be a skinny nigga he had hell of muscles. The nigga had the nerve to be short too not to mention the little man syndrome we were damn near the same height. He had a tattoo covering his chest and it was too dark for me to read every single one of them but with time I planned on not only reading them but licking every inch. His goatee was always lined fresh and his cornrows stayed in the same style no matter when he got them done. He rocked them in the same style as the rapper Lil Flip from back in the day. This man was the truth and there was no denying that. I stopped admiring his beauty and crawled in bed resting my head on his chest and drifted off to sleep.

I was sleeping so peacefully I didn't realize someone was outside my door knockin on it until my phone started ringing and a damn near fell out the bed trying to grab it only to realize it wasn't on my nightstand where I normally place it before bed. Then I realized it was in my living room on the couch where I left it the night before. I looked over and didn't see Dame in the bed anymore. I had to have been out of it in order for him to get up and me not even wake up. On another note why didn't he at least wake me up to say bye, shit even thank you would've been fine. I'm normally a light sleeper but those drinks and that dick put a bitch in a coma. I ran down the stairs with my bra and a pair of shorts I grabbed out of my laundry basket when I got out the bed.

"Just a minute I yelled" while grabbing my phone before looking out my peep hole to see Lee and Netia standing there looking agitated. I opened the door and turned around and headed for my couch. My head was spinning, and I knew it was about to be a long day. I had a hangover out of this world, and the night prior was every bit of worth it.

"Well hell Miss I'm going to call yawl after my date, but just now waking up at three o'clock in the afternoon." Lee said while closing the door behind her.

"Shut up bitch I was drunk by the time I got in last night and now I have a hangover like a motherfucker." I was resting my head on the back of the couch and trying to keep my eyes open because every time I closed them, I swore the room was spinning. I got the sudden urge to throw up and I ran upstairs making it to my bathroom just in time. I started singing to the porcelain gods. I swear I must have thrown up everything I had eaten over the past week then dry heaved for what felt like forever. I brushed my teeth, washed my face, and headed back down the stairs feeling much better but still a slight headache. It's funny how throwing up can make you feel so much better.

"Damn boo you ok?" Netia asked with a concerned look on her face.

"Yes, I feel much better now, I still have a slight headache but nothing like it was before."

"Good bitch no fill us in on how your date with the mystery mate went." Lee said sitting Indian style on my floor with a bag of Grippos in her lap.

"Let just say long story short that nigga is the King of the Jungle and a bitch ain't never had dick like that before in her life. He should have a crown specially made for his dick. Shit his momma should have named him two heads and three legs. He should have an award for the type of skill he possesses. I could go on and on."

"AWWWWWWW" The both of them screamed covering their mouths. The looks on their faces were priceless.

"Damn bitch I don't even want to hear none of the details cause a bitch ain't had none in months. The only king of the jungle I have been getting any action from are the toys from Lion's Den. But I'm glad it was good" Netia said giggling.

"Shit you got me ready to get the fuck up and walk out that door and head to Coby for a round two" Lee said laughing as well.

My phone chimed right as I was about to head to the kitchen and cook something up for us to eat. I knew it was a text message from the alert tone. Looking at the screen display, his name sent chills up my spine and caused a huge grin to spread across my face.

Dame: My fault for up and leaving you this morning ma I had business to tend to, but I locked you bottom lock.

Me: It's coo I assumed you had things to do. Thanks for locking the door behind you.

Dame: Shit I ain't want nobody to come in there and steal none of the tight ass pussy while you were sleeping. LOL

Me: LOL you're crazy!

Dame: Na that's you miss lady! Your young ass got some fire ass pussy though real shit. A nigga was regretting not getting up in that shit this morning after I left.

Me: Don't worry it's here waiting on you whenever you decide to come back for seconds.

Dame: Oh, is that right!

Me: Of course, it is!

Dame: That's what's up imam hit you up a little later ma! Have a nice day Erin.

Me: You as well I'll talk to you later.

As soon as I placed my phone on the counter, I started grabbing shit out of the cabinet to prepare something for lunch a bitch needed something on her stomach and quick. We were sitting in my living room eating fried chicken wings, green beans, with Velveeta shells and cheese watching reruns of Snapped when my phone rang. The screen read Unknown so I answered it curious as to who I would be.

"Hello" I answered the phone with a mouth full trying my hardest to sound normal.

"Hello?" the woman on the other end of the line greeted me with an attitude.

"Who is this?" I asked

"No who is this?" The caller asked back with the same attitude and tone she said hello in.

"You called my phone, I'm the one who should be asking the questions" I said now matching the caller's attitude.

"I'm calling your phone because your number was in my man's phone and I wanted to know who the fuck it was texting my baby dad." Her response caught me off guard because the inly nigga I had been texting had been Dame and I had just got done texting him not long ago and if she had been in his phone she would have saw he was texting me about my pussy so she was calling her self-checking the wrong person.

"Look I think you may have the wrong number or person. Have a nice day hun" I said to her!

"No bitch I don't have the wrong person or name you been texting him all week and I'm just now deciding to call you because he didn't come home last night and that's unlike him so I'm checking this shit before It gets out of hand. Dame! Does that name ring any bells in your head hoe?" As soon as I heard her say his name, I ended the call. There was no way in hell this bitch had been monitoring our calls all week or could she have been. I knew that nigga was too good to be true. With a face, body, and dick like that I should have known it came with an extra-large plate of drama on the side. I didn't know Dame had a baby shit he never brought it around to any of Lee's family gatherings or parties. Shit I didn't even know he had a woman, but I guess that's to be expected. A part of me felt dumb as fuck for giving that nigga some pussy on the first night only to turn around and have to deal with his baby momma not even twenty-four hours later. I can't lie I felt a little defeated because Dame is four years older than me and I'm sure the bitch was probably his age and just my luck they probably had years of history and time put into their relationship just because that's how it always plays out. Instead of telling my girls the shit that just happened I decided to continue to play along as if the caller had the wrong number out of fear of sounding stupid after just bragging about how good this nigga put it down and now getting private calls from his women.

"Who was that?" Netia and Lee both asked at the same time.

"Some lady who had the wrong damn number, I should've known because it was private. Don't nobody ever call my phone private."

"Oh ok, I was about to say what hoe we bout to go have to beat the fuck up before I head off to college this weekend." Lee was now standing up headed to the kitchen to put her plate in the sink.

"I was kind of wishing it was a bitch talking sides ways because I got some frustration, I need to let out I told yawl I been fucking all of Lions Dens toys! Shit!" Netia said with a hint of disappointment in her voice and we all fell out laughing. That's one thing I love about my girl them hoes always down to ride no matter what and no matter how pretty we all are we all get down and dirty and ain't scared to fuck any bitch up who steps out of place.

The remainder of the day we all lounged around my apartment watching TV and listening to music. The girls even helped me clean up and fold clothes that had been sitting in laundry baskets for the entire week. Days like this was what I was going to miss the most about Lee moving away. I tried to stay busy the whole day but thought of Dame, the dick he had put on me, and his baby mom kept racing through my head. As bad as I wanted to text him and say something, I didn't want to sound pressed or even childish because we had only fucked once, and I wasn't his woman. It was my choice to give him some ass and we were only friends but damn if he had a whole bitch at home, he should have told me that from the jump instead of pretending to be single as a dollar bill. I decided I wouldn't be contacting him until he reached out to me first and if he didn't then I know what it really is. Can't miss out on a man that you never had, nut that dick I did have, and I would for sure miss that if he never called or texted me again.

4

LEE

$\mathcal{I}$ had only been away at school in West Virginia for a week and already I was feeling home sick. Tomorrow was the first day of classes for fall semester and I couldn't even get my mind prepared for my first day of college because of missing Coby. Although we texted and talked on the phone all day since I had left it wasn't the same. I was so used to seeing his face and Facetime just wasn't enough for me. Other than missing my boyfriend like a sick puppy everything else seemed to be going good. The campus was huge; it took me the first two days to locate all of the buildings my classes were located as well where practices would be held. I don't see how people gain the freshman fifteen referring to weight if you had to do so much walking in order to get where you had to go. If I was the type to ride a bike, I would have definitely gotten me one and it wouldn't be a waste of money considering the distance I had to walk on a daily basis. My dorm room was small yet cozy, I had decorated my side to my liking, it felt more like home with the decor and pictures I had in place than I originally thought it would.

My roommate Kelly was also a freshman. Kelly didn't play any sports, so she had a lot more free time on her hands than I did. She also didn't have any ties back home to keep her in the dumps about being away. Kelly was from Kentucky and she was every bit ready to live and enjoy her college experience to the fullest. Every night since we had been here, she was out; either attending campus events or some party. Kelly was a very pretty girl standing about 5'3', she was thicker than a snicker and I'm talking the king size ones. Kelly weighed about 180 pounds and most of that went to her ass and titties, she had to be about a 38 DD, she had a small stomach that was hidden under those big breasts of hers. She is light skin with green eyes and rocks her hair in bundles that are 24 inches and longer. I had yet to see her real heart but with us being roommates in due time she would evidently reveal if she was bald headed or wore the weave by choice. She had the prettiest smile and I could tell that she was used to being hot shit where she came from because of her infatuation with herself and looking at herself in the mirrors. Unlike myself Kelly grew up in a single parent home and didn't come from much, she had told me one of the first nights we were here that she was used to working to get everything she wanted even if that meant using what she had to get it. I took that comment as her basically telling me she was a gold digger and would fuck to get her way, I wasn't judging shit you get it how you live and if that's how she chose to live her life that that was her business. From the looks of her things she was very well kept and had plenty of designer things so I would have never guessed that she didn't have a set of rich or well-off parents sitting back at home taking care of her. Kelly had a 2012 Silver Jeep that she had just received as a graduation gift this past May from her mother, she took pride in it because she said it was one of few things her mother had ever purchased her besides food and shelter. Like every other night we had been here she was once again gone and even though I thought she would be turning it in early I had gotten a text from her saying she would be late because she had changed her schedule so the first class wouldn't start until after noon. After receiving her text message, I decided to hop in the shower and lay it down so I would be rested for the next morning. Gathering my things, I was thankful for the dorm room that I had chosen to live in. Unlike the traditional dormitory we didn't share one bathroom with the entire floor instead each room had its own full bathroom compliments of the building being a formal Holiday Inn hotel. After my shower I decided to send Coby a text message.

Me: Goodnight baby I'm about to lay it down. I love you and I'll talk to you in the morning.

Coby: Good night Pooh, enjoy your first day I'll call you after my first class. Oh and of course I Love you 2.

Once I read his message, I placed my phone on the charger and made sure my alarm was set for 8 o'clock in the morning, giving me more than enough time to get dressed and head across campus to my English 101 class. Laying down I daydreamed about how my first day would go and before I knew it, I had drifted off to sleep.

I had been in school for almost two months and things were going pretty good for the most part. My classes were a breeze and practice weren't as hard as I expected it to be for college basketball. I had even met a few new friends in a few classes that I would have lunch with or study with from time to time. The guys down here are all corny as fuck, I mean it's not like I'm checking for any of them but those who were checking for me were for sure shot down because they weren't even of my caliber even if I want with Coby. Kelly wasn't doing as well when it came to transitioning into college life. She was struggling with all of her classes and I would blame it on the amount that she partied. I swear for every homework assignment she had two drinks. This girl even had a mini bar hidden under her bunk, which was clearly against all campus rules and regulations. I think the freedom of doing whatever you wanted whenever you want including class was too much freedom for a person like Kelly, but she will manage. Coby was due to come down here for the weekend and I couldn't wait until my last class today so I could start my weekend off right. Two months may not have seemed like a long time but to me it felt like two years away from my baby. My girls Erin and Netia were coming next weekend and I couldn't wait to kick with them either. Which reminded me I had to talk with Kelly about making plans for next weekend to make sure we show the girls a good time, since she knew all about West Virginia and I only know the pathway to my classes, practice, and the grocery store. This morning Kelly had told me she would be going back home to spend some time with one of her guy friends and wouldn't be returning until Sunday night, so Coby coming today was perfect timing. I would have the room to myself and didn't have to worry about having my man around the next female in such a small space. We could have gotten a hotel room if Kelly wasn't leaving but Coby declined stating he wanted to see what our campus was all about.

I was practically running down the stairs of my dormitory to get to the student parking lot where Coby was waiting for me. Coby had just called and told me to look outside! To my surprise he was parked right beside my car and standing outside in the front of his car with a dozen roses in hand and a teddy bear from the looks of it. My dorm room was on the third floor so It wasn't like I could just walk out the door and run into his arms, the elevator was taking too long for my patience, so I opted to take the stairs instead. Thank goodness I was in shape or this would have been one hell of a journey to run. Reaching the back door, I got a second wind and took off into the parking lot until I was in Coby's arms. His smile matched mine when he could see me running towards him with my arms reached out in front of me.

"Baby!!!!! I'm so happy to see you! You just don't know how much I've missed seeing your face and being in your arms" I squealed as Coby embraced me with one of the tightest hugs, he had ever given me.

"Aww Pooh I'm just as happy to see you if not happier! And If you missed me even half as much as I missed you than I can imagine" He said with a slight giggle. Coby handed me the flowers and teddy bear he was holding, and I couldn't do anything besides blush and get butterflies inside like this was the first time he had ever greeted me this way when it wasn't.

"Thanks baby! How sweet, you didn't have to bring me any gifts seeing your face and being this close to you was good enough for me"

"I know but I didn't want to come empty handed all the way down here to see my Pooh. Plus, it's nothing big just a little gesture of my love for you."

"So, what's the plan babe?" I asked while still holding on to his waist now looking up into his eyes.

"That's up to you I'm in your city now, I'm doing whatever it is you want to do."

"Ok cool, but for the record this is NOT my city! BuckTown all day baby don't act like you forgot" I said putting a little base in my voice to let him know I was serious when it came to repping my home town, causing him to laugh at my silliness.

"Oh, ok well excuse me! But you know what I meant"

"Well let's go grab something to eat first. I haven't eaten since lunch because I was so anxious about your arrival. Now you're here I'm suddenly starving" I said rubbing my stomach with my free hand.

"I'm with that, I'm kind of hungry myself what do you have a taste for?" Coby started rubbing his stomach as well at the thought of grabbing something to eat.

"For real I have a taste for my momma food, ain't nothing like a home cooked meal when you're away from home for so long but since that's not even an option let's do Logan's Steakhouse."

"Ok baby let's take your things and my bags upstairs so I can drain the main vein really quick then we can go" Coby was no adjusting himself in his sweatpants and the sight of his bulge from the print in his grey sweatpants sent an instant reminder to my body how long it had been since I felt him inside of me causing my panties to instantly get wet.

After taking my gifts into the room, Coby's bag, getting him a visitor badge and temporary parking permit, we were now on the freeway following my GPS to our location for dinner. The ride to the restaurant Coby made fun of me having full access to my car and still not knowing my way around a city that had been my new home for the past two months. I told him I wasn't trying to get to know the city because my focus was basketball and my work for the time being and I would have more than enough time to learn my way around this dead ass town.

We were sitting at the table looking over our menus waiting for our waiter to come back with our drinks so we could put in our orders. When the waiter came back with our drinks in hand and placed them on the table we were more than eager to order our food, our stomach was sending us signals by growling on que at the same time when she asked were we ready to order and we all began to laugh.

"Ladies first." Coby nodded his head towards me motioning for me to place my order first. I loved Cody and he was always such a gentleman towards me. He always opened doors for me, allowed me to walk in first, and held my hand in public. I looked up at him and smiled before placing my order.

"umm let's see! I'll have the onion rings for an appetizer, The 8-ounce sirloin well down with broccoli and mash potatoes with brown gravy and a side salad with ranch please." The waiter raised her eyebrows like she was surprised that I had ordered that much food being as small as I was. Coby snickered because he was used to my hardy apatite.

"And for you sir the waitress turned her attention to Coby to take his order."

"I'll take an order of hot wings for my appetizer with bleu cheese dressing. The barbeque rib tips with a loaded baked potato and side salad with bleu cheese as well."

"Will that be all?" The waitress asked, looking at us both.

"Yes" Coby and I said in unison

"Ok I'll go and put these orders in right now and your appetizers should be out shortly."

Over our meals we talked and caught each other up on how school had been going for the both of us. Coby's phone was ringing so much during our dinner he had to power it off to stop it from interrupting us. I never had any reason to question him or be insecure over the course of our relationship, so I brushed it off assuming it was only his boys or teammates trying to see what was going on with him.

I hadn't realized how tired I was until Coby was shaking my arm lightly waking me up letting me know we were back at my dormitory. I guess this week being so full of exams and practice on top of dinner had me overly tired. Since we were now back to the place I now could call home I had to get so energy because there was no way I was going to have my boyfriend drive three and a half hours to only have dinner and me fall asleep on him. I had plans for him and his little friend in his pants tonight. It was well overdue. I hadn't had any dick since the night before I left for school.

"Baby I'm about to hop in the shower really quick. The remote to the TV along with the TV guide is on my desk beside my laptop." I grabbed my towel and headed toward the personal bathroom in my room to freshen up.

"Ok, don't take too long in there and make me have to come looking for you" Coby stated with lust in his eyes.

"I won't but then again that doesn't sound too bad after all" I said matching the mood I could see he was in.

As bad as I wanted Coby to come join me in the shower since we had yet to take a shower together, I needed to hurry up because I couldn't wait much longer to feel him inside of me. Once out the shower I lotion my entire body with Pear Glaze and wrapped my fresh towel around my body, instead of putting on the night clothes I had originally placed in the bathroom to put on. Walking out into my room the only light I could see was from the TV and the screen from Coby's phone. The TV was turned all the way down and I could hear music playing on Coby's phone. As soon as I saw Coby sitting on the edge of my bed naked as he was born with his hard dick in hand I dropped my towel and seductively walked over to him. I was trying so hard to be cute and sexy I hadn't realized Coby's shoes in the middle of the floor and damn near broke my neck when I tripped over them. I had to catch myself on the computer chair before I fell face first and made a fool of myself ass naked. Coby and I both busted out laughing when I regained my balance and finished walking over to him.

Putting my hand on the side of his face and leaning down to kiss him on his lips Coby slipped his tongue inside my mouth and we allowed our tongues to tangle only causing my center to get wetter as we made love with our mouths. I pulled back and got down on my knees and pushed his legs apart, so I was sitting right in between them. I gripped his hard dick and jacked him off a little before putting my lips on the tip of it. I looked up into Coby's eyes and he pushed my head down to take more of him in. although I wasn't just ready to take all of him inside of my mouth I figured he couldn't take any more of the waiting game and was ready to get this shit started. I started suckling and slurping on as much of his dick that I could take inside of my mouth. Coby was my first so of course his dick was the first and only dick I had ever sucked. I wasn't no pro but I did enough to get the job done as well make him go crazy with the moaning so that was all that mattered. Coby started moaning and holding the back of my head aggressively fucking my mouth at a rapid pace. With every thrust I could feel the tip of his dick hit the back of my throat. I tried to pull back some because I was gagging way more than normal but the grip he had on my head didn't allow me to. Right when I felt his dick begin to jump inside my mouth he stopped and grabbed me up from the floor and laid my back on the small XL twin size bed spreading my legs apart. Coby took no time placing his dick at my entrance and putting all of him inside of me in one swift motion. I let out a lite grunt at the pain, it had been two months and I had to get back use to fucking him it was like I was a virgin all over again. After a few strokes, the pain was now taken over by pleasure and I could feel my juices building up and spilling out of me.

"Shit Pooh this pussy feels so good! Damn I miss this shhhhit" Coby moaned

"Baby I miss this dick too! Oh my...... Coby, just like that baby! Uggghhhh it feels soo good baby!" I could feel Coby hitting my spot causing my orgasm to be in the near future if he continued.

"This my pussy! This my pussy? Huh?" Coby was moaning and asking was this his pussy, but the pleasure was so great I couldn't mutter anything at the moment.

"Ye..Ye.. yea...yess.. muuuhhh ugghh ohhhh" I was moaning and trying my hardest to reply but it wasn't coming out properly. Coby looked me in my eyes and grabbed me by my throat and applied pressure.

"I asked was this my pussy Lanice! Are you giving my pussy away? This is my pussy!" Coby's lustful eyes didn't show as much lust and he appeared to be getting agitated that I hadn't answered him correctly. He had even called me by my first name which was out of the ordinary, but he never stopped stroking his dick inside of me while asking the question. Thrown off by his actions the orgasm that I was so close to having ran far the fuck away and my pussy was now drying up because I was unsure what the fuck had just happened. Trying to loosen his grip from my neck so I could breathe and answer him, I was able to finally give him the answers he was originally looking for. But it was too late the mood was now ruined.

"Yes, Coby this is your pussy and no I'm not giving it away to anyone but you baby" I said barely over a whisper. I decided to answer him in fear he would grow upset with me again for nothing. The sex that was feeling so good was now something I was wishing would be over with sooner than later.

"You better not be Pooh! This my pussy and it feels so good! Ohhh shit I'm bout to nut. AGGGGGGHHH I love you!" Just that fast he was back calling me Pooh like he hadn't switched up on me just moments prior. Unlike any other time when Coby would pull out and let his nut cover my flat stomach, he held my hips and let it all go inside of me.

"I Love you too Coby" I said dryly, sat up and headed to the bathroom to get right back in the shower to wash off the filth I now felt all over me.

While in the shower I could hear Usher Lovers and Friends playing in the room, but I toned it out with my thoughts. Coby had never made me feel the way he did tonight. I Couldn't believe he was even questioning if I was really down here fucking and giving up my body to just anybody. The person I just given my body to wasn't the man I normally have sex with and what he just did to me was, fucked me, it wasn't passionate like the normal sex we share. I felt used and dirty. Coby had never even questioned my loyalty to him let alone bluntly accused me while inside of me. To top it off he nutted inside of me as if he was marking his territory for the next man to know it was his in case.

By the time I got out the shower Coby was sound asleep stretched out to the best of his ability in my little ass twin size bed snoring as if everything were ok. He was still naked and had only attempted to put on his socks. As bad as I wanted to just grab a cover and sleep on Kelly's bed, I opted to just make a spot on the floor beside my bed. As soon as my head hit the pillow the thoughts of what had just taken place clouded my head again and a few tears escaped my eyes and landed on my pillow. This was the first time Coby had ever done anything to hurt me or my feelings and I wasn't used to the feeling my heart was now experiencing.

The rest of the weekend went by as a drag and Coby carried on in his normal moods and things seemed to be back to normal. I shook what happened Friday night off as a mistake and decided to push it to the back of my mind and not mention it with hope it would never happen again. Cody was now about to head back home and as bad as I wanted him to stay, I knew he had to attend class the following Monday just as I did. Walking Coby to his car I began to get sad, other than Friday this whole weekend had been all about me and catering to my needs of missing him. He made sure to give me his undivided attention. He hadn't even powered his phone back on from dinner Friday night. I was ok with that because I honestly didn't want any interruptions or distractions.

"I love you baby and drive safely, make sure you call or text me as soon as you get back to Columbus." I said as I wrapped my arms around his waist and hugged him.

"I love you too Pooh, and I'll make sure to let you know as soon as I get back make sure you get in there and get that homework done that you didn't complete. I'll be seeing you soon." Cody said before leaning down to kiss me. I puckered up and after pecking my lips twice we allowed our tongues to say the rest of our goodbyes for us. I let go of Coby's waist and stood back as I watched him pull out of the parking lot. I watched his car until I could no longer see him anymore. It was time to get ready for my week ahead of me and finish up the homework I had neglected for the weekend but not before calling home to talk to my mom first. I missed my family so much and couldn't wait to see all of their faces upon returning home for the upcoming holidays.

Dupree

Y'all may have already heard a little bit about me and know that I'm one of Kris' close friends, but let me formally introduce myself, I'm Dupree Kels but my boys call me "D". I'm 24 years old and currently bleeding the block trying to get rich or die trying. Sike nah I'm bullshitting with yawl; however, I do hustle to get it by any means necessary, but I also have a 9-5. I work with my pops doing construction for the city of Columbus. I was born and raised in Columbus Ohio and grew up in a single parent home, with just my younger brother Dame and my Father. Although it was only my father who provided for us he worked his ass off to make sure we never wanted for nothing but as my brother and I got older we started hustling to take the load off my dad and have been getting to it ever since. Our mother died back when we were kids from cancer and that left my pops Dame Sr. to raise up. I know you're wondering if I'm the oldest then why is my brother the Jr. Well the story was told to us that my parents were expecting a baby girl instead of me and were surprised when I came out with a third leg, so they named me on the spot. They both chose Dupree after my Grandpa because he was the only one who kept telling my parents they were having a boy from day one. I'm guessing back then the ultrasounds were pretty shitty quality and they must've mistaken my dick for my leg cause ain't no way in hell they could've missed it or confused it with no coochie. I graduated from high school and earned a Technical Certificate for construction while attending a career center during high school, so I've been in the work field since I crossed the stage. My pop always asked that no matter what we got ourselves into that we made sure we always had something legal to fall back on. Back in the day before my mom passed away my pops used to be the man in the streets but when my mother died, he had to settle down and become a full-time father. My mom made, my pops promise before she died to get out the game and raise her boys and not let us fall victim to the system because of his own foolish actions. Pops kept his word and no sooner than we laid my mom to rest he started working full time and left the streets alone.

I'm a laid-back type of dude for the most part and I surround myself with only my brothers. Yeah, I only have one biological brother and that's Dame but Kris been my nigga since tighty whiteys and hot wheels so blood couldn't make us any closer. Many people look at me as a ladies' man 'cause I do in fact have a way with the ladies but settling down right now just ain't what I got in mind, unless it is with Renee but since that ain't happening I'm just doing me. I'm 24 with no kids, no baby momma drama, nice whip, my own spot, and cash so of course women want a nigga like me. I'm not the type of dude hopping from female to female crib and depending on a female to survive. Shit not to mention I'm one sexy ass chocolate nigga. Nah I'm not conceited or anything, but I know what it is. I stand 6 feet, 200 pounds of course my body is nice a nigga work construction and build shit for a living, dark skin, keep a nice crispy fade with wave that will make you sea sick, I keep my goatee trimmed and lined real nice, and the ladies say my lips remind them of that old cat LL Cool J.

Kris, Dame, and I were headed to some new club for a grand opening and to celebrate my little brother Dames 23rd birthday. I know the nigga only a year younger than me but his actions and the way he acts makes me feel so much older than him than I really am. Don't get me wrong my brother ain't no little nigga but he still got a whole lot of growing up to do. When we pulled up to the club the line was wrapped around the building and from the looks of the outside crowd this muthafucka was about to be jumping tonight. Instead of riding around looking for a parking spot Kris pulled up and let Valet park his whip. Although we all had transportation whenever we stepped out, we rode together just out of habit unless we had a lady friend with us. When we stopped out the car looking like three walking licks the ladies were eye fucking us as we skipped right pass the line and entered the club. I opted to rock an all-white True Religion jean outfit with a black True Religion V neck tee shirt with white writing, accompanied with a fresh pair of high top white on white air force ones, my diamond pinky ring, and Gold chain. There was no way in hell I would be posted in no long ass line that was wrapped around the building and same for my niggas. Since we were in the streets of course we knew the bouncer, so we slipped him a bill and we were in the club in no time. The inside was looking just as live as I assumed it would from the crowd outside. Instead of heading straight to our VIP section that was reserved for the evening we decided to walk around and check out the crowd first. After getting a good feel of the crowd and our surroundings we headed to the VIP section and got comfortable. Some fine ass redbone approached our table and I assumed she would be our bottle girl or should I say personal bartender for the night. Shorty was cold but I could tell she was an all-around THOT from her approach that I wanted no parts in. "Hey fellas what can I get yawl tonight?" She asked in the softest voice. I could tell by the way Kris was eyeing her, he ain't give a fuck how she sounded or looked like a THOT, by the end of the night she would be added to his collection. Kris was the type of nigga that didn't give a fuck if a female was a THOT or not if he wanted her, he would bag her without a second thought, it's a surprise this nigga ain't running around with hell of kids by now. After ordering a bottle of Patron for Myself, Hennessy for Kris, and Cîroc for Dame we sat back and enjoyed the music until the little red bone returned with our bottles.

"Aye man peep shorty who came to help us, shorty cold as fuck but I think I used to fuck with her sister back in the day" Kris said.

"Shit I wouldn't doubt it nigga knowing you" I replied. There was no telling, fucking around with Kris. I was dead ass serious when I said that nigga gives no fucks.

"Fuck it bag the bitch and have a threesome with her and her sis" Dame said, and we all let out a little laugh. Dames ass was a handful and didn't give a fuck.

"Haaaaa my nigga I might just do that shit. If I'm correct I think her name is Ebony or some shit like that and her sister is Jerin." Kris was rubbing his chin like he was thinking hard about if that was really their names or not. As the little red bone approached our table, she was holding two of the three bottles we ordered in the air with sparklers followed by another redbone holding up the third bottle with sparklers and a bucket with our ice. The glasses were already neatly placed on our table, so it was time to get our night started.

"Aye ma I ain't catch your name!" Kris said to the little red bone. He knew like I knew she never mentioned her name when she first approached our table, so he was going to force her to reveal her true identity.

"I'm sorry my name is Ebony, I thought I introduced myself already! If I didn't again, I apologize. " Bingo was written all over Kris' face as he nodded and smiled at her with a look of approval. Ebony gave him a seductive smile and walked away with a little more pep in her step making her little ass jiggle in the little shorts she was wearing with her fishnet stockings and combat boots. I don't know where the hell these damn bottle girls be getting their sense of fashion, but they be putting that little shit together alright.

We were turning up in our VIP section and pretty lite by the middle of the night when I noticed Renee walking toward the bar across the room. I noticed she was with three other females, but I couldn't tell who they were from the distance between us. Renee was standing to the side and looking straight ahead so she didn't even notice I had peeped her. Since Renee and I weren't public with the little shit we did and had I wasn't going to approach her instead I turned my attention back to the unknown female that was twerking in front of me and trying her hardest to keep my attention. Our VIP section was filled with random females as always trying to be chosen. Dame was drunk as fuck and enjoying himself from the looks of if, and I was happy my little bro was enjoying his birthday. As soon as I reached for my bottle to take another drink, Kena, Dame's baby mom was sashaying her ass over into our section with her sidekick Ciara. Kena was a coo chick but she took her and my brother's relationship to the head at times and forgot she was his baby mom and that's it. Her sidekick Ciara and I fucked a few times but nothing more, Ciara was sexy as hell but had the worst attitude problem, so I had to cut off her supply when she started talking out the side of her neck. I guess Dame saw Kena just as well as I did because he removed the unknown female that was sitting on his lap and stood to greet Kena.

"Happy birthday Baby!" Kena shouted as she wrapped her arms around Dames neck as if she was his woman. Dame embraced her with a tight hug around her waist and I could tell he was feeling his drinks because Dame didn't normally play that touchy feely shit in public, in fear Kena would take that shit to the head and think they were more than they really were.

"Hey D!" Ciara said as she took a seat next to the table helped herself to the only bottle that was left sitting unattended on the table. Instead of greeting her back I simply gave her a head nod. Kena was now in full blown turned mode and was twerking the shit out of my brother to the point he had to lean up against the wall to support his weight so he wouldn't fall back.

All my diamonds shine cause they really diamonds
Bad bitches in line, they be really trying
They ask me if I'm high
I say really really
Got money on my mind
I say really really
I look like I been balling cause I'm really ballin
I won't apologize
I'm not really sorry

Kevin Gates "Really Really" was booming through the club speakers causing me and my niggas to turn it up even more, because we knew we were really really doing our thang and it was no secret to those around us. We were all rapping every word to the song and meaning each and every word that came out of our mouths. It had been a minute since we had been out on the scene and even from our VIP section, we were shutting shit down. Whenever we did go out, we always went hard and showed out so tonight would be no different. I was surprised when I saw Renee in our VIP section greeting her brother with a hug with Netia, Erin and some other brown skin girl in tow. It was weird as fuck seeing them all without Lee by their side, but little sis was away in college doing her thang so I ain't mad at her. Renee was looking good enough to eat right about now in a skintight red dress showing off all her curves causing me to give her the evil eye. Renee knew better than to be rocking something that short showing off her legs and ass then come over into our section as if she wouldn't get confronted about her appearance. As soon as Kris released her from his embrace he started talking shit about what she had on right on cue as if he had read my mind, she only waved her hand in his face and continued to take a drink from the glass she had in her hand as if she paid him no mind. After the ladies greeted us all I caught Erin eyeing Dame and from the looks of if she wasn't feeling him or Kena. Whenever Erin saw Dame, she gave the googly eyes, but this look was something different. Dame hadn't even looked up to greet them back; he only nodded his head and buried his head further into Kena's neck as she was now giving him a lap dance. I knew Erin had a thing for little bro but from what I knew they never took it anywhere so I made a mental note to ask Dame what was up with the way she was eyeing him all of a sudden with anger. Netia, Erin, and the chick they were with all took a seat and joined the crowd we had in our section. I was so focused on Renee and what she had on, I forgot all about shorty in front of me until she asked me why I had been so anti-social with her. I mean shorty had been all in my face the entire night, but the truth was I was high as fuck and feeling this Patron so me ignoring all her advances wasn't intentional. After putting my bottle on the table I took a seat on the sofa and shorty made sure to have a seat right along with me but on my lap this time, I guess this was her way of making it known that she wanted my undivided attention. Instead of pushing her off I decided to just let the shit ride and enjoy my night. It's not like Renee and I are together anyways, so this was in no form or way me trying to be disrespectful towards her.

RENEE

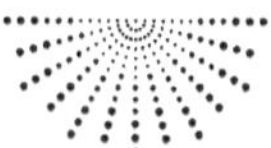

As bad as I wanted to ignore Dupree and the little rat ass bitch, he had all in his face I couldn't, that shit was irritating the fuck out of me. Rather we were together or not. That shit wasn't sitting right with me, but there was nothing I could say because we never really talked about us being exclusive nor were we public about anything going on between the two of us. I tried to sit where I wouldn't be able to pay attention to what was going on with Dupree and the chick, but I couldn't stop myself from looking over and catching little glances of the two. The chick was obviously flattered that he was giving her the time of day because she had a huge smile plastered on her face, Dupree on the other hand was hard to read. I mean he was smiling but he always smiled so that told me nothing. Erin's entire attitude had changed from the moment we stepped into the guy's VIP section and she laid eyes on Dame. Dame hadn't even noticed we were in the section because he was so into the bitch, he had all in his lap practically fucking him with her clothes on. I knew she always had a little crush on him but the look she was giving him was a death stare, it's none of my business but I'm going to make it my business to find out what's going on between the two of them tomorrow morning as soon as she sobers all the way up. There was some girl sitting across from me giving Dupree the same stare Erin was giving Dame but she tapped her friend that was on Dames lap and told her she would be back, so I assumed she wasn't feeling Dupree entertaining the girl either and couldn't stand it any longer. Netia and Milan were both busy eyeing the other guys that were in the VIP section to pick up on anything that was going on around us. Milan is my home girl from work, we rarely kick it outside of work because the two of us are both always busy but whenever we do it few and far in between. It's almost like the DJ senses our mood because the throwback from Trina started beating from the speaker.

"Shawty said the nigga that she wit ain't shit,

Shawty said the nigga that she wit ain't shit,

Shawty said the nigga that she wit ain't shit,

Shawty said the nigga that she wit ain't shit "

Erin was feeling her drinks and the song more than I was. She had started dancing and pointing her fingers as she rapped along with Trina. Damn reality was really sitting in along with my Cîroc, the nigga that I was with ain't shit and now I'm seeing neither is the nigga I was fucking on the side. I was taking away from my thoughts and I realized that the girl that was dancing on Dame was now eyeing Erin as if she had a problem. Erin was facing Dame and the girl so there was no disguise that she was rapping the song to him. The song was coming to an end and Drake's HYFR started playing as the chick's friend reentered the VIP section in a better mood than she left with. Oh, the girl must've got some liquid courage or some balls upon her friend coming back because she was now on her feet and staring Erin down as if she was on some bullshit. I tapped Netia and gave her the eye letting her know some shit was about to go down because Erin was in no form or way a scary bitch so it was only a matter of seconds before she whooped that hoe all around this damn section. The friend walked over and whispered something in her ear, and it must have added some fuel to her fire because she was now walking towards Erin.

"So, you must be Erin huh?" The chick said with attitude writing all over her face and in her tone.

"Yep sure am and who the fuck are you?" Erin asked, matching the chick's attitude.

"Ha, oh you ain't know I'm Dames baby mom Kena!" My mouth damn near hit the ground and I could tell her comment caught the rest of the girls off guard as well, but Erin was playing it off well.

"Ok and what the fuck does that have to do with me?" Erin asked her acting as if the last comment didn't affect her, but I knew it was just as much of a surprise to her as it was to me because we never knew anything of Dame having any children.

"Listen bihhhh...." She was cut off by Dupree grabbing her up by her arm and pulling her in the opposite direction.

"Yeah ok! Let that bitch know this won't be the last time she sees me and next time it's over with for dat ass" Erin said to Kena's friend and pointing in the direction Dupree has dragged her to before walking away. We all turned and walked away following Erin, not allowing the friend to even have time to respond.

Waking up with a fucking migraine out of this world let me know just how drunk I got the last night. The last thing I remember was us walking out of the guys' VIP section and everything following that is a blur. I reached over on my nightstand beside the bed to grab my phone so I could see if I had any missed calls or text. Looking at the notifications on my phone screen only pissed me off. I was hoping Dupree would have called or at least tested considering he paid me absolutely no mind last night but to my surprise he didn't. The only name besides my mother's was Mark of course. Mark had blown my phone up all night, my guess is he didn't catch the hint the first five times I didn't answer his calls. Scrolling back through my messages I see that I originally texted him first telling him I was horny and missed him. I could only palm myself on the forehead and mutter Damn under my breath. That had to be the liquor texting him because I had clearly decided that I was done with Mark and wasn't turning back this time around but my guess is the rejection from Dupree last night along with liquor combined caused me to turn right back to what I had just walked away from. I go to get a better grip on my feelings when I drink because last night's carelessness could have caused me to wake up next to Mark which I truly didn't need or want. I'm thankful I passed out and didn't stay awake long enough to allow him to come over because I would definitely be kicking myself in the ass right about now. Instead of returning my mother's calls I decided to jump in the shower and head over to my parents' house. Hoping out of bed my phone started ringing and I could tell it was my sister by her ringtone.

"Well hello my Lee!" I greeted my sister with so much excitement in my voice. I truly missed the hell out my little sister yet I'm so very proud of her because I didn't have the courage to move away from home and chase my dreams in fear of failing. Lee is my little sister, but she is so much wiser than her age. If you didn't know Lees actual age you would never guess she is as young as she is from her persona.

"Hey Nae! I'm on the way to practice. I don't have much time to talk but I heard it was going down last night. Do I need to make a trip back home to handle some shit?" Lee's tone matched my excitement yet was very stern and serious about the question she asked. Lee was the complete opposite from me. She would slap a bitch in the drop of a feather whereas I hated confrontation, I avoided any drama by any means. Lee's temper was so much like our mothers whereas I was more laid back like our father.

"Hunny you don't even know the half, well then again you might" I giggled. "Long story short something is going on between Erin and Dame I'm guessing cause Dames surprise baby momma was ready to fight over lord knows what. If it wasn't for Dupree pulling her drunk ass away Erin was going to give it to her ass right, there in the VIP area we were seated." I rushed and told my sister a quick version of the story.

"Yeah Erin didn't go too much into detail but she is definitely messing around with Dame and from what I hear ol' girl been on some bullshit now for a little minute now I'm not sure how long but last night was the first time they came face to face. I told Erin I would talk to her more about it when I come home this week for Thanksgiving break and if the hoe needs to be handled for her to at least try to wait until then when I'm home."

"Damn I ain't know for sure but now that shit makes sense that Erin and Dame been doing some shit behind closed doors, well shit I guess his baby mom did have a reason then. I need to know the details or at least what Dame has to say about all this because last night he was to fucked up to even realize what the fuck was going on around him."

"Yeah, we gon' see what's up, but I'm at the Rec now so I'll either text or call you a little later. I love you and Kiss Sanai for me."

"Ok Love you too, and I sure will. Talk to you later" We ended our call and I sent a text to Erin and Netia telling them to come by my house later for dinner and some Mimosas. After sending the text I headed to the bathroom to get my shower and dress like I was doing prior to my sister calling.

After getting dressed I headed to my car and just as I was locking the bottom lock to my front door, Mark's ass was pulling into the parking spot next to mine. Thank goodness I was leaving, and I could rush him off. Me not answering his calls wasn't enough so he just had to pop up. I wish his ass would stop with all that poppin up shit, there was no reason to come to my apartment he doesn't have my daughter so what is his excuse today besides the fact of him trying to be nosey. I hit the unlock button on my keypad to unlock my car doors attempting to appear to be in too much of a hurry to stop and have small talk with Mark. Unfortunately, that didn't stop him. Mark stepped out of his car and walked over to the driver side of my car and waited for me to get into the car, leaned down and motioned for me to roll the window down.

"Renee what the fuck do you be on man? You really starting to confuse and play with a nigga and I don't like this shit." Mark wore the look of frustration all over his face and his tone of voice didn't hide it any.

"Mark what are you talking about, I'm not playing any games with you." I couldn't even look him in the eye because I knew he was referring to my text messages from last night.

"Renee don't play stupid you know exactly what the fuck I'm talking about. How you never answer my calls or text messages unless

I have Sanai then you randomly texted me out the blue talking about how you want to be fucked and miss a nigga. Then when I try to come through you ignore all my calls. Instead of calling me back this morning like a normal person would do after they see the missed calls and text you get up and continue with your day as if you ain't see none of my calls or text messages from last night." I could see exactly where this conversation was about to go and honestly, I wasn't trying to go there with Mark today, shit my head was still light weight hurting.

"Look Mark, I'm sorry about texting you randomly last night I was drunk, and I shouldn't have texted you to begin with. It wasn't my intention to play with you, shit honestly, I don't even remember texting you. I came home and passed. When I woke up this morning the first thing I did was hop in the shower and now I'm headed to pick up my baby, so I hadn't even taken the time to even read through your messages." I lied but I didn't want to agitate him anymore than he already was, all I wanted was for him to walk back to his car and allow me to leave and get on with my day.

"That's the childish shit I be talking about! You're confused! You don't even know what you want. One minute you want to fuck with a nigga the next minute you taking back everything you said." Mark was cut off by my phone ringing. Instead of looking at the screen I kept eye contact with him while answering my phone.

"You at home? I'm bout to come through really quick I'm in your area meeting my nigga." Dupree said without giving me the opportunity to answer his question. Dupree never stopped by during the day because of his work schedule so as of lately it had never been a problem for him to call or stop by if he was in the area without proper notice. But today his timing couldn't be anymore off.

"Yeah I'm home but I'm about to leave actually. We can meet up later if that's ok with you. I'm headed to go pick up Sanai and grab something to eat" I replied in a low tone hoping he didn't sense the nervousness in my tone, because that would only cause him doubt if what I was telling him was the truth. The look on Mark's face told me that he was about to start with his drama. No sooner than Dupree asked where I was headed to Mark opened his big ass mouth as I expected.

"Nae who the fuck is so important that you being all rude and shit. Tell whoever it is you will call them the fuck back" Mark said with venom dripping from his voice. I stared into Marks eyes and wish I could have smacked the fuck out of him right then and there. If I knew that he wouldn't fuck me up in return, I damn sure would have smack him.

"Yep you got it. I see you got company. I was actually turning into the lot when I called but it's coo, I'll get up with you later. Go ahead and get back to your nigga." Just like that he ended our call and I could tell her was pissed by his town and remarks. Dupree was so disappointed; he ended the call before I even got the chance to respond. Aside from the fact that his actions last night had pissed me off to the max, the last thing I needed was for Dupree to think I was back fucking around with Marks sorry ass which is not the case. As bad as I wanted to call him back and just tell him to come on over so I could have the opportunity to explain myself I opted to just wait until I spoke to him later to see exactly where his head was at. I also know for a fact Marks ass wouldn't be leaving if he didn't see me actually pull off and leave first. After throwing my phone over into the passenger seat I turned to look at Mark to see if we were now finished with the conversation we were having prior to the call. I'm sure he could see the look of irritation written all over my face, if it wasn't evident before Dupree called, I know for sure it was now. The conversation Mark and I were having prior to Dupree's call was definitely over with now. Mark and I weren't even together anymore yet he was giving others the impression it was more than it really was, and I hated that shit. It's almost like he was intentionally making it hard for me to move on because over his own selfish reasoning. I applied my foot to the brake and put my car in reverse and prepared to leave without verbally telling Mark.

"Damn Renee you just bout to pull off just like that with me still standing right here, without even allowing me to finish what we were talking about before your phone call? I'm not even going to ask who it was; just know you can't keep playing with me like I'm some little as boy toy or some shit Renee. I got some shit to do then I'll hit you up. Hopefully, you answer the phone if not, I'll be back by here later." Mark stated in the most serious tone.

"Look Mark, I'm trying my hardest not to be rude, but I told you I was leaving when you walked up to me. I have somewhere to be and I'm trying to get there."

"Ok you on your bullshit again today I see, it's coo Renee. I'll be by later to pick up my daughter" he said as he turned to walk away." No matter how much I still loved Mark inside it was best for us to be apart he had done too much wrong and it was finally time for me to begin to live my life and find happiness outside of him. Plus, Mark could front all he wanted to pretend to have matured, but I know that was just his way of getting me back in his good grace.

"No need for you to return Mark. Have a good day." I said before rolling my window back up and pulling out of the lot.

When I got to my parents' house of course she was in the kitchen as always preparing something. I swear this woman needed a show of her own on the cooking channel. My mother's recipes were always the bomb. There wasn't a dish she couldn't make and if she didn't know how she would tweet up some shit and figure it out. Of all my years of living I don't think a day went by that my mother didn't prepare at least one meal. Even on the days she would be sick or not feeling well she still made it her business to make at least one trip to the kitchen. Sine Sanai was asleep when I arrived, I decided to stick around my parents until she woke up. Sanai was the sweetest baby but if you interrupted her nap or slumber, she would turn the fuck out and I knew better than to get her up and cranky when I still was feeling a little tired from the night prior. Instead of joining my mother in the kitchen for small talk or my father in the living room to watch his shows I decided to head upstairs to my old room and take a nap.

Laying across my queen-sized pillow top mattress I decided to call Dupree before I drifted off into my nap. I didn't know exactly what to say or how to start the conversation off but I didn't want him to think I was lying earlier or that there was something else going on being the reason I didn't allow him to come over. The phone rang three times before Dupree answered right before I assumed the call was about to go to voicemail. Dupree answered in a nonchalant tone. I asked him what he was doing and if he was busy. Instead of telling me no like he always does whenever I call or reach out to him, he simply said yeah, I'll get with you later. His background was a little loud, but I knew Dupree wasn't at work because he never worked on Saturdays but if he said he was busy then he was busy. All I could do was say ok and once again he ended the call without a goodbye or seeing if I was finished talking to him.

I rolled over and damn near fell out the bed. I had forgotten I wasn't at home and was actually in my bed at my parents' house. I was more tired than I thought, and it was now nighttime. I had slept the entire day away and missed hell of calls. Of course, Mark was amongst the calls, Netia, Erin and a couple unknown calls. I was disappointed when I didn't see a call or text from Dupree, but this was only showing me I needed to just fall back completely on him and let the shit we had ride. As bad as I wanted to deny it I had fallen harder for Dupree over the last couple of months and if I was confused about how I felt about him before I was for sure now that I loved him and he was the person I wanted to be with but I was too scared to admit it and face what everyone would say if they found out about us. Netia texted me and told me that she and Erin were just about to chill over Erin's crib and would get up with me tomorrow and I was ok with that because there was no way I would be going home to cook anything and it's damn near 6 o'clock already.

When I got downstairs, I could tell my daughter must have woken up and turned my parents out there were toys everywhere and she was now laying on my father watching TV so peacefully. My mother must have already gone upstairs to prepare for tomorrow. She never stayed up really late on Saturdays because she had to be at church the following day. I went over closer to my dad attempting to grab Sanai off of him and prepare her to go home but he held her tighter and told me to go ahead. She was ok to stay with them another night. As much as Sanai was a handful my parents surprisingly never got tired of her being over. It seemed as if since Lee left for school they wanted Sanai more and more, and I think that's because they were so used to having at least one of their children in the house on a daily basis and they were actually lonely without any of us in the house. I didn't mind them helping out because with the workload that I had taken on lately I needed all the sleep I could get whenever it was available. As bad as I wanted her to just go ahead and stay, I wanted to spend so quality time with her, so I promised to bring her back in a few hours.

After grabbing Sanai from my father's tight embrace, we headed to Magic Mountain so I could spend some quality time with my baby girl instead of just simply going out to eat. I be damned if I didn't run smack dead into Dame, the bitch from last night that I'm assuming is his baby mom with a little boy that looks like a spitting image of Dame. The little boy had to be about a year old, not much older than Sanai, I couldn't believe that this was the first time seeing him. Dame had never mentioned a baby and as close as he was with Kris you would think that would be something, we would all know about. I was trying to act as if I didn't see him but when he gave me a smile and waved at me, I knew my cover was blown. There was no way Dame would ever see me and not acknowledge me considering he was practically like family. When the girl looked in the direction Dame was waving her attitude instantly switched up. If looks could kill someone would be not only burying me but my daughter as well. I simply gave her a smile and kept it moving. I order us a pizza combo since we still hadn't eaten anything, as we were sitting down and getting situated I noticed Dames baby mom walking towards my table talking on the phone but I didn't see Dame with her so I'm assuming she was trying to be funny by even coming anywhere near me without the company of Dame and their child. She made sure to make sure I heard her talking on the phone with one of her friends. "Girl yes Dames as put it down last night, that nigga ain't going nowhere I don't know why these hoes even try to compete, but how was your night with Dupree enough about me." I wasn't going to even give her the satisfaction of knowing I saw her until she mentioned Dupree's name. Now I was wonder who the fuck her friend was and if she was the bitch that was all in his face. No Dupree isn't my man, but I couldn't help but still feel some type of way knowing he even entertained the next female. Ol girl looked back at me and gave me a devilish smile; that's how I knew exactly what she was doing. Although she didn't know if I was talking to either Dame or Dupree, she for sure one of the girls I was with last night was fucking with both and I would run with the little information I heard. Luckily for her I'm not the messy type and I had my daughter with me or else I would've called Erin right up to her to be just as messy as she was being. Once we ate and I could tell that Sanai was becoming restless I decided it was time for us to head home, it was damn near closing time anyway, so Sanai was more than tired and ready for bed. Hoping in the car I grabbed my phone out of the middle console to check for any missed calls or text and I'll be damned if not one call or text was from Dupree. The way he rushed me off the phone earlier I was at least hoping for a returned call or something but there was nothing. I couldn't believe he had the nerve to really be acting this way after the stunt he pulled last night. I guess I'll just be the bigger person and call Dupree. He answered on the third ring and I'm glad he did because I was for sure he was about to allow my call to be greeted by his voicemail.

"What's up Nae?" He greeted me nonchalantly.

"Hey what you doing?" I said nervously.

"Shit bout to head to the crib and call it a night."

"If you're not too busy Would you like to come over and watch a movie?"

"I just told you I wasn't doing shit, but you sure you want me to come over? Sure, your nigga ain't coming back?" I knew he was only being sarcastic, but I couldn't help but get offended by his comment.

"First off, he isn't my nigga and no he isn't coming over, so are you going to come?"

"yeah let me run home really quick to change clothes and I'll be through I'll text you once I'm outside."

"Ok, I'll see you soon"

"Bet"

I looked back to check on Sanai and she was sound asleep before I was halfway to my parents' house. She had so much fun running around and playing in the balls. Looking at my little sleeping beauty I still can't believe my baby will be one in less than a month, this time is flying by. Once I dropped Sanai back off to my parents and headed home. Mark had called a few times while we were at Magic Mountain. I called back before I got home just so he wouldn't pop up but to my surprise he didn't answer. Soon as I stepped foot in my apartment I headed upstairs and hopped in the shower. After my shower I threw on a pair of leggings and a tank top. Instead of wrapping my hair up I placed it on the top of my head in a messy bun. No sooner than I sat down on the couch I heard my phone going off all the way upstairs. I ran up the steps to get the phone and it was Dupree letting me know he was outside via text. Instead of grabbing my phone I left it on the charger and headed back downstairs to open the door for him.

Dupree wasted no time kicking off his shoes and grabbing the remote to the TV and selecting a movie off of Netflix. He didn't greet me with a hug, kiss or even a simple hello like he normally would. I could sense his attitude from his demeanor and the energy he was giving off. I didn't like the side of Dupree he was showing towards me over the past twenty-four hours. Instead of rushing and addressing the elephant in the room I decided to just join him on the couch and play it coo for the moment. If he wanted to talk about how he felt, I would wait until he spoke up. I didn't want to piss him off any more or run him off because I really wanted his company tonight. Once he picked some scary movie, I cuddled up next to him and grabbed the small throw that was on the couch to cover my legs. Dupree didn't even wrap his arm around me like I expected him to, he just adjusted his position so he wouldn't be uncomfortable. After the previews for the movie were over, he asked me to grab him a bottle of water. As I was walking back from the kitchen, I looked over to see him lighting his blunt and taking a few pulls before placing it back into the ashtray. I laid back in the position I was prior to getting him something to drink and prepared myself for the movie.

"Look Nae, this shit we got going on between us is starting to fuck with me for real ma." I sat up and faced him while folding my legs

Indian style giving him my undivided attention. I was hoping he wasn't getting ready to cut me off because that's the opposite of what I wanted from him especially at this moment in time.

"Ok Dupree what's up bae, talk to me." I said in a soft tone.

"Nae you got my heart for real and there's no need for me to sugar coat this shit. I can't stand to see you with that nigga when I know he means you or Sanai no good. I'm not about to sit here and shit on the next nigga but I've been around to witness it all no matter if you tell me everything or not, I see shit. I can't even lie or pretend that when you're with him it doesn't do something to me. I know we ain't together and you're not mine publicly, but I feel like you are. This secret shit and hiding what's going on between us ain't goin last much longer. I'm not trying to make you choose because if you feel the same way I do it wouldn't even be a question on who it was you would choose but what I will say is I'm not about to sit back and continue to play the background if you still entertaining this nigga." My heart was smiling yet still torn because although I knew Dupree was feeling me I didn't know it was this deep and as bad as I wanted to let go of Mark. A part of me still was in love with the man he once was.

"Dupree, I have strong feelings for you too, but I'm scared that this that we have here won't last long if we make things official. I have history with Mark and at the moment we aren't together, but he is still the father of Sanai and I can't just cut him off completely. I don't want to lose what we have between the two of us over him. I just don't want to get hurt again and this is all coming from my heart." I was looking into Dupree's eyes so he could see that everything I was explaining was just as sincere as what he had just told me. No matter how hard I started into his eyes I couldn't tell how he was taking anything I had just said. His face wore no expressions or emotion, so it was making it very difficult to determine his mood.

"Look beautiful if yawl not together and you want for us to continue what we have. You got to learn to deal with him on the strength of Sanai and Sanai alone. There's no reason he should be in the picture if it has nothing to do with his seed. I respect you got history with the nigga but if you not trying to have a future with him what's the point? But honestly, I respect you wanting to take shit slow and not get hurt so I'm gonna leave it alone I told you how I feel so there's no questions on that shit. I'm going to keep it one hundred with you. Me hurting you would never be my aim and you should know that but I'm going to let you figure this shit out just don't take too long to do so Nae."

"Ok Dupree." I couldn't say anything else because he had honestly left me speechless by the fact he was sitting here on my couch telling me everything a woman would want to hear and up until this point I could've sworn this is what I wanted to hear but couldn't accept it. A part of me wants to take it slow but the other part still felt Mark and I would work out in the future. I needed time to think no matter how stupid it may sound I needed time to think this shit out clearly before deciding on anything. Dupree laid back and reclined in his seat and I laid my head back on his chest. This time he places his arm over my shoulder and before I know it, I was watching my eyelids instead of the movie. I woke up in the middle of the night and was in my bed with Dupree's arms wrapped around my waist. When he felt me move, he shifted with me and kissed the nape of my neck before drifting back off to sleep. I felt so at ease in his arm and held onto his arm that was resting on my waist before I rejoined him in dreamland.

Mark

"Mark I can't fucking believe you! How could you burn me again? This is the second time this year. It doesn't matter how many times I forgive you and take you back you continue to do the same shit over and over. What is it that I'm doing wrong that makes you creep on me? I just don't understand I'm home all day, I cook, I clean, I even help you with your daughter whenever you ask me for money. Not to mention I'm pregnant again and you don't even want me to keep this baby" Nyla was yelling at the top of her lungs crying about some bull-shit I really didn't care to hear right about now. I had tuned her out five minutes ago. There was no way I could sit here and actually listen to her annoying ass cries and complaints. My mind was in a totally different place. Nyla and I had been fucking around now for about a year and she wasn't lying when she said she takes me back through it all. If it was something wrong a nigga could do to a woman, I had done it to her. The only thing I hadn't done was put my hands on her. As bad as Nyla made me want to fuck her up, I knew that would be the straw that broke the camel's back, and I honestly needed Nyla. Nyla may have not worked but she was stable and overall a great woman she just wasn't the woman I wanted to be with. When Nyla and I first started fucking around she got pregnant and it was right after Renee had Sani so there was no way I could allow her to keep the baby. Shit I hadn't gotten used to having one child let alone two, plus financially I couldn't afford two kids at that moment. So needless to say, hi convinced her to get an abortion, but that didn't stop me from fucking her raw nor had she started birth control like she swore she would. Little shit Nyla would say and do let me know she deep down wanted a family with me. Starting a family with Nyla was something I didn't want. I was trying to get my family back with Renee.

Shit me burning her was a surprise to me as well her. The first time I didn't know who burnt me but what I do know is I had burnt her and Renee both. This time I was for sure it had to be the new little young bitch I fucked raw. I only fucked her once but that's all it took was one time. That bitches pussy was so warm and wet but I thought that it was just her reaction to me but now I know that bitch was having pussy issues, I hadn't had any side effects so I'm glad Nyla did find out or I would still be clueless. "MARK are you even fucking listening to me? All you fuckin care about is yourself. How would you feel if I did this type of shit to you that you do to me and then ignored your ass when you tried to talk to me about how you felt? Huh? Answer me!" Nyla continued to rant and yell, but I couldn't take it anymore. This wasn't he shit I came over here for.

"Look Nyla I'm out I'll be back tomorrow and hopefully your attitude is better by then. I came over here to spend time with my woman and this is the type of shit I get in return. And stop saying I burnt you cause my dick clean so who else you been fuckin. Huh? You answer me!" I knew Nyla was loyal to a nigga and that pussy belonged to me, but I couldn't just sit back and not say anything or that would only make me appear to be even more guilty than I already am. I grabbed my Wheat Timberlands and cell phone and to head right back out just as fast as I came in here.

"Mark, I know you're not leaving! What is it? what am I doing that is so wrong or bad you can't stand the fuck up and be real shit just man up and stay home with your WOMAN and be faithful. That's all I'm asking from you. Is that too much to fucking ask for? Every time you feel some type of way you leave and ignore me as if I don't even exist instead of staying, talking, and working shit out like we are supposed to do." Nyla was crying and being all fucking dramatic for nothing. This whole pregnancy was causing her to really erk the fuck out of my nerves. I don't know if I'm going to be able to tolerate this shit the entire pregnancy and I sure as hell hope it doesn't get any worse than this. I came over here horny but now I'm bout to leave out of here annoyed and turned off. I could go to my mom's crib but I'm not trying to do that either. Times like this I wish Renee wasn't on her bullshit so I could go to the place I once called home. Renee hasn't been as standoffish as she normally was lately, but she still wasn't allowing me to stay at her house nor get any pussy. Sanai's first birthday party is coming up so hopefully with preparation for that I can get her to let her guard down some. When I got into my car, I decided to send Renee a text message just to let her know that she is on my mind.

Me: Good night Nae! I miss you and my baby girl. I just wanted to let you know that I think about yawl all the time and I love yawl both.

Renee: I miss you too at times but so much has changed between us Mark. I will always love you. We just need this time apart because things weren't right and that's not healthy for Sanai. Good night to you too by the way.

Me: I'm sorry for all the bullshit I put you through and I'm trying to show you I'm working on a better me. You're right Sanai didn't need to witness us arguing all the time. Can I come take yawl to breakfast in the morning?

Renee: Yeah that's fine I'll call you in the morning. Good night.

Renee shocked me by being so open and honest with me about how she felt without being rude. She had been real adamant about letting me know she was done and didn't want to work things out but just her response tonight had me feeling like there was still some hope left. In all honesty a nigga couldn't help but smile when she said she missed me too and is willing to go to breakfast with me in the morning. I know Renee loves me, but I also know I'm not right for her, but I can't see her with another nigga. I refuse to sit back and watch the next nigga be all up in Renee's face and around my baby girl. Instead of going to my mom's I decided to go back into Nyla's and just try to calm her down because she is still the mother of my unborn and I don't need her stressing the baby out causing complications. I used my key to walk in and I could hear Nyla in the room crying her eyes out. As bad as I wanted to walk right back out the front door I just took a deep breath and did the right thing and that was to walk into the room and comfort my side bitch that was just recently promoted to my baby momma.

The look on Nyla's face showed fear and surprise. I guess she was so into her feeling she hadn't even heard me walk into the house let alone walk into the room. I hated seeing her upset, in the beginning Nyla was perfect hints she made it this far being one of my main females I fucked with. Shit most of my belongings were here at her house. I practically lived here but I would never completely move out of my mom's until I knew I was ready to settle down because bitches switch up too much and too fast for me. There weren't any words needed between the two of us because the tension was so strong it would only cause even more friction. I removed my shoes first then undressed and laid in the bed next to her. I grabbed Nyla around the waist and pulled her near to me before reaching on the nightstand and turning off the lamp. I wrapped my arms around Nyla's small frame and rested my face in the crock of her neck. I could feel the tension she was holding inside being released as she got comfortable in my arms. Nyla placed her hand over mine and whispered, "I love you Mark and I'm sorry". Instead of saying what I wanted I just replied by telling her I loved her too and I was sorry as well. I closed my eyes and before I knew it sleep took over me.

The smell of bacon and eggs along with the warm, relaxing feeling of Nyla's lips wrapped around my dick woke me out of my deep slumber. She caught me off guard with this trick out the hat, but that was just like Nyla to do whatever it was I wasn't expecting. Nyla was a good bitch in all honesty, she was bad as fuck and very submissive, but I just can't get Renee out of my heart enough to love Nyla the right way. Nyla is beautiful inside and out; she Filipino and black so she has an automatic exotic look about her. Nyla stands about 4'11 weighing no more than 125, she has no tities but her hips and ass are perfect for her small frame, she has the straightest teeth, with one dimple on her left cheek, she rocks her hair bone straight and its damn near to her ass, her beautiful brown slanted eyes are what caused me be drawn to her in the first place. When she started waving her tongue on my dick causing a tingling sensation I was taken away from my thoughts and brought back to the situation at hand. Nyla moved her tongue in ways I never knew were possible. It was like she could do acrobatics with her tongue effortlessly. Nyla sucked and slurped until I felt like she was about to suck the soul out of me. The way she was looking up at me in my eyes was about to cut this moment short. I don't know how much longer I can hold out with the sounds, feeling and looks she was delivering. She took my dick out her mouth just long enough to ask me if I forgave her for last night and went back to work. She knew what she was doing and that I had already forgiven her the moment I woke up with her head between my legs. I couldn't even answer her I just lifted my body off the bed with my elbow and started fucking her face back. "Hummmm, shit...Yeah suck that dick just like that! ummmm" before I could give her proper warning I was releasing inside of her mouth and it only caused her to suck faster and harder while still keeping eye contact with me. Nyla sucked me dry literally when she finished my dick didn't show any evidence of my semen or slobber that she was just covering my dick with. She had swallowed every drip drop.

Nyla removed herself from the bed and headed to the kitchen. When she returned, she had a tray in hand and a smile on her face. She had prepared blueberry pancakes, scrambled eggs, bacon, fresh cut fruit and a smoothie. After the nut I had just bust my stomach was growling at the sight of the meal she had prepared for me. I wouldn't mind waking up every day for the rest of my life to breakfast and head but if only if it was from Renee instead. I can't say I don't love Nyla because I do and little shit like this is the reason why but I'm still in love with Renee. That plate didn't stand a chance with me, my plate was clean within minutes. When Nyla removed the tray from my lap and headed back to the kitchen, I grabbed my phone out of my pants pocket and headed to the bathroom. Normally a morning piss was the first thing on my agenda but not today a morning nut and full gut came first. After pissing I washed my face and brushed my teeth before checking my phone. I had three missed calls from Renee about two hours ago. I was damn near noon and I'm sure she was pissed that I hadn't answered when I was the one who wanted to go have breakfast. It was no longer breakfast time and there was no way I could eat any more after the meal that I had just demolished. Hopefully, she wouldn't be too resistant to having lunch or even possibly dinner with me because I planned on getting right back into the bed and relaxing for a little while longer. Nyla didn't work so If she wanted to lounge around all day and cuddle she would do just that. I shot Renee a quick text message telling her I had been at the hospital with my mom all night and I didn't have any service. I asked would she be willing to reschedule for dinner later this evening. She replied back within seconds telling me that was fine and that she hoped my mother would be ok and to let her know if we needed anything. I knew Renee wouldn't question me when it came to my mom and she would also feel sympathy because she works in the medical field so anything revolving around a person's health touched her heart. I powered my phone off before leaving the bathroom and heading back into the bedroom to relax for the next few hours.

I woke up a little after five and that was perfect timing. That nap was so peaceful I got all the rest I needed and without any interruptions. I rolled over to see if Nyla was next to me, but she wasn't. Nyla had left a note on the nightstand informing me she was over her parents and would be home before late and to text her when I woke up. Instead of texting her like she requested I decided to power my phone on and text Renee telling her I would be by to pick her and Sanai up at seven. I hoped in the shower and got dressed for my evening. I didn't want to dress to fancy or dress down too much, so I was rocking an all-white Ralph Lauren button up with a pair of black Levis and a pair of all white Retro Jordan ones. I had recently gotten a fresh lineup, so I was looking clean as hell. For me to a light skin nigga I wasn't the pretty boy type, don't get me wrong your boy is fine but not much of a pretty boy weighing 255 pounds of solid muscle I'm much bigger than you average dude and standing six-foot-tall I could easy past for a sports player but I'm not at all. I work odd jobs here and there as security at clubs around the city but that's about it. Sports ain't and have never been my thing. Seeing Renee walk out the house with Sanai in her arms brought me back to reality. Renee is cold even when she isn't trying, and Sanai's little face melts my heart. Sanai is such a sweet baby, it's still hard for me to believe at times that I even have a daughter. Renee had on a pair of dark denim jeans with a tan fitted shirt and a pair of tan flat boots. Her hair was brushed back into a ponytail with a part in the middle, she didn't wear much makeup but her nude lipstick looked perfect on her dark brown skin. After placing Sanai in her car seat in the back of my car Renee joined me in the front seat and fastened her seat belt. Renee didn't have any idea on where we were headed, and I wanted to surprise her by taking her to BRIOs in Easton. Renee wasn't really picky nor did she require much to make her happy, but I was in the process of trying to prove I had changed so the basic Applebee's dinner just wouldn't cut it tonight.

Over dinner Renee and I actually had a great time. She silenced her phone, so I did as well. If she wasn't going to allow any interruption neither was I. I knew it was only a matter of time before Nyla was going to start blowing my phone up anyways since I never texted or called her once I woke up and left the house. We talked about Sanai for most of our dinner, I opted not to bring up us trying again in fear it would cause a mood change and I didn't need that right about now. When Sanai started getting cranky I took that as my sign to bring the night to an end because my baby girl was getting restless plus Renee mentioned to me that she had work at 7 am in the morning as well so I knew I had to get them home. Tonight, would only be the first of many date nights and dinner with the two of them. I drove Renee home, carried Sanai into their home that we once shared and kissed my baby girl goodnight before placing her into the crib. Before leaving I made sure to give Renee a kiss in the forehead and tell her I would call her in the morning.

6

ERIN

hen I walked outside preparing to head to work saying I was livid would be an understatement. I couldn't believe the mess that stood before me. My blood was boiling, and I couldn't believe someone would be so fucking childish and petty to fuck with my damn car. My car may have not been the newest or the best-looking car, but it was my fucking car that I paid for with my hard-earned money and nobody had the right to fuck with it. That's one thing you don't do I don't give a fuck how pissed you are don't touch a bitch car, that's the way I make my money and if you fucking with my money then you better be expecting payback. There were well over three dozen eggs splatter all over my car and from the looks of it there was cooking oil poured on top of the splatter's eggs. This shit was going to take hours to get off completely not to mention the shit stinks. I pulled my phone and called into my job letting them know I wouldn't be making it today due to car problems. I didn't explain what kind of car troubles but shit they didn't need to know that. The next person I called before going into the house to change so I could head out and get my car cleaned was Dame. I don't have a problem with any females shit I don't have problems with anybody so the only person who could have done this would have to be that wack

80

ass baby mom of his. The fact that m y car was the only car bothered let me know the person was targeting me. In a complex full of car who would just random choose my little ol car out of at least 25 cars to fuck with. Dame didn't answer when I called so I sent him a text message instead of calling back.

ME: Since you can't answer your fucking phone, I'm just going let you know that you and your ugly ass baby mom got me all the way fucked up. I would hate to have to beat the breaks off that hoe, so I suggest you get your ugly ass over here as soon as possible.

Dame: I'll be there in less than five minutes.

I didn't even reply. I just changed out of my work clothes and slipped on a pair of grey yoga pants and a black tee shirt with my all black mid top Air Force Ones. Since Dame said he was on his way here I decided to sit on the front room couch and wait for his arrival before gathering any cleaning materials for my car. Not even two minutes after I sat on my couch, I heard Dame knocking on my front door. I hopped up and answered it not even giving him the time to say a word before I started going in on his ass. "I know you see the mess on my fucking car, and I know you whack ass baby mom had something to do with it. I'm not even tripping that she upset with me cause that bitch already got an ass whopping with her name on it from the shit she pulled at the club but to fuck with my car instead of simply knocking on my door is what's going cause her to get it even worst. What type of weak bitch fucks with my car but won't confront me? Your weak ass bitch that's who!" I screamed. "Wait calm down shorty, I ain't doing shit but I will pay to have it detailed. How you go know it was my baby mom for sure anyways?" Dame had the nerve to be serious when he asked that last question. "First and foremost, I didn't even know your old ugly ass had a baby mom until that night of your birthday when the hoe tried to jump stupid. But to answer your question I have no problems nor had any problems until after I started fucking with you. First it was the prank calls and stupid shit like that now this." I said pointing out my front room window to the direction in which my car was parked. "Now we both know you mad but we both know a nigga far from ugly" Dame said with a slight smirk on his face. "But I didn't tell you about my baby mom because I hadn't told anyone about her. I tried to apologize a million times about that night since then and the first time I get to talk to you for more than two minute you're over here cussing me the fuck out and ready to body me over some shit I had no control over. If I would have known she was starting shit with you and playing on your phone I would've been put her in her place, but you chose to keep that shit from me, and I don't know why." I couldn't help stare at him a begin to feel bad for blaming all this on him I know Dame is a coo dude just because he has always been even before we started messing around but I was still pissed that my car was looking like someone allowed the entire chicken coop to take over my car and drop all their loads on my car. "Look Dame I don't have time to deal with this petty type of shit nor will I continue to tolerate the bullshit she trying, I let her ass get a pass the night of your birthday but this is it the next time she pulls some funny shit I'm beating that bitch the fuck up no questions asked and there nothing you can do about it." Dame walked over to me and his cologne took over my nostrils causing my panties to become soaking wet. I hadn't fucked since the last time me and Dame had messed around and that had been well overdue. Dame grabbed me by my waist and pulled me close to him and whispered in my ear how he apologized, and he only wanted to fix this minor shit between us. I agree I wanted to fix things between Dame and I because I had been wanting him for so long and once I finally got him it seemed like poof her comes some random baby momma no one knew about to come up and mess everything up in only a matter of days. As bad as I wanted to fight the temptation and feeling I was having with dame hold me I couldn't. I honestly wanted to forgive him and be back in his arms sooner than now, but my pride and ego wouldn't allow me to forgive him so easily. Dame started caressing my ass and pulling at the waistband of my yoga pants I didn't resist because I wanted it just as bad as he did. Right there in my living room with my blinds open and all I allowed him to undress me completely and caress over my entire body while still standing in the middle of the front room floor. Once I was completely naked, he pushed me back onto the couch and spread my leg and dove headfirst into my juice box. The feeling of his tongue alone was enough to make me cum from anticipation, but I couldn't give in so soon. Dame was fucking me with his tongue like he had a point to prove and I was accepting of it. Palming the back of his head and grinding my hips unto his face even hard caused him to devour me like he was feasting on his last meal on death row. My moans were so loud I'm sure my neighbors would have been pissed if they were home. Dames moans sounded so sexy with the mixture of the slurping sounds of him tasting my juices. "Dame I'm bout to …. I'm bout to cum…. Oh my God. Dame I'm cumming" I screamed in between gasps of catching my breath. Dam licked his lips and stood to his feet. He started unfastening his belt and I could tell by the bulge in his jeans he was already at full attention and ready for me to put his man's down. I tried to assist him and prepare to suck him dry but when he pushed my hands out the way I looked up at him with disappointment in my eyes. I only wanted to make him feel good like he had just done for me. "Nah ma I want some of this pussy, a nigga been missing you" that comment made me blush and before I knew it Damn had my legs in the crocks of his arms and was plunging his rock hard dick into my juice box. Dame was fucking me like we would never fuck again, and I was enjoying every minute of it. I couldn't believe I let this man stay in the doghouse so long pretending I would be done with him. There was no way I was letting him get away with me so easily without a fight rather we were together or not. It's almost like Dame was reading my mind because right on cue he asked me "Ma this pussy belongs to me, you mine now right no more of the bullshit between us, right?" "Yes, Dame just don't play with my feelings" "I won't ma I got us" he said, and I believe every word of it without even a second thought. I don't know if it was the dick or sincerity in his voice, but I was gone and convinced. When I felt myself-coming to my climax, I could tell Dame was about to release his seeds as well and it felt good to cum together now that we were an item. I didn't even protest because the feeling was so great not even caring that he didn't heave on a condom and allowed all his seeds to swim freely into my body.

After the fuck session we had in my living room we showered together and got dressed. I wanted to ask Dame how serious he was about us, but he didn't give me the opportunity to before he spoke up first. "Erin I wasn't playing about you being my girl now, so I'm going to fix this shit with my baby mom and make sure she chills the fuck out. I don't need yawl two going at it and her holding my son over my head. I'm bout to take this trip out of town with my nigga for a couple hours and I'll be back here tonight. Here goes some money to get your car detailed and have a little bit of fun with some retail therapy when you're done to calm your nerves I'll talk to you later ma" Dame said all in one breath before kissing me on the lips and heading downstairs to head out. When I looked at the money he placed in my hand I was in shock. He had given me well over five hundred dollars knowing damn well my car wouldn't cost that much. I was all smiles. If this was the treatment he offered for being with him I could damn sure get used to it and there would be no way I would fall short of being the woman he needed me to be.

I sent out a group text letting the girls know I was in dire need of a quick ladies' session or meeting after I got my car detailed and for them to meet me at my house around four. When Netia and Renee texted me back saying they would be there I was happy. Lee even text back saying to call her and place the phone on speaker phone since she couldn't physically be there made me smile. I loved the fact that I could always fall back and depend on my girls for support more than just physically, but mentally, spiritually, and even financially if need be. Having a history and bond with a group of loyal females is rare nowadays so I cherish the relationship I have with the three of them. When I got my car back it looked like It was brand new off the show-case floor they had out done themselves when they cleaned my baby up and I was thankful that Dame was more than willing to foot the bill for his baby mom's stupidity.

Pulling into my apartment complex I could see Renee's car parked next to my spot where I normally parked. When I got out the car I rushed over to her car and greeted not only Renee but Netia with a hug. After saying our hellos, we all headed into my apartment. Instead of preparing something to eat, I ordered up a larger pizza, a side of hot wings, a foot-long sub and a two liter of Pepsi. There was no way I would be slaving over no stove when I needed to update my girls on what had been going on in my life and my plan for revenge.

By the time I gave my girls the run down on who it was I had been fucking on the low and why I chose to keep it a secret they weren't as in shock as I expected them to be. I guess my behavior the night of his party was a dead giveaway in something going on between the two of us, I hadn't realized I had made it so obvious. When I told them about the prank calls and the bullshit that took place with my car this morning, they were both ready for war and Renee wasn't even the fighter type. Renee made a few phone calls and was able to find out exactly who Dames baby mom was not only including her first and last name but her address as well. Once we were done discussing the plan, we formulated for the revenge on the hoe Kena we ate our food and headed out to the pet store.

It was still kind of early, but it was dark and I'm sure the hoe wouldn't be leaving anytime soon. Dame was out of town and would be returning to my place once he did return. Being it was a Monday night I knew there weren't any clubs or events taking place that would cause her to need to leave the house after ten thirty. We all placed on our latex gloves and medical mask to block out the smell. Renee popped the trunk and grabbed the large box that included 100 miniature frogs. The frogs were kept in the box without any air or ventilation in the trunk since we purchased them earlier today so the majority of them were dead at this point. We each grabbed a handful and placed them all on Kena's all white Nissan Maxima. Since they were dead the shit that accumulated in the box throughout the day only made these little slimy, stinking ass reptiles appear even worse than it really was. We had covered her front windshield, back window, and the top of her car to the best of our ability. Our work here was done but not before Netia Spray paint with bright neon orange on the hood of her car "Stank Hoe"! Thank goodness he lived in a single house or we may have been caught by her neighbors and that would have not only been embarrassing but a fucked-up situation. Riding back to my place we all laughed at the thoughts and ideas on how she would react once she witnesses the sight of her car tomorrow. I couldn't care less how she felt about what I did because she started the shit but I for certain would be the one to finish it every trip she came for me. The girls and I sat and chit chatted for a little while before the both headed back home, and I cleaned up the place before Dame returned. Lee was pissed she missed out on our fun tonight, but she couldn't believe the shit we had just pulled. Lee even had the nerve to ask if we had taken pictures, but we were so caught up in our handy work no one even thought about snapping a few pictures now I wish I would have just so I could have something to look back on and laugh.

It had been about a month and a half since Dame and I had made it official and everything had been going great, I had no complaints about him or us. To finally get with you crush from childhood on up and actually be happy is a good ass feeling. Your girl had been feeling herself on a whole new level. It was no secret we were in item and Dame even allowed me to post pictures of us on social media and I knew that was something he didn't get into because he wasn't an "Social" type of nigga. I hadn't had a period since two weeks before Dame and I had our little sexcapade in my living room the day we made up and every fiber in my body knew I was pregnant. Good thing I wasn't throwing up or showing any symptoms or Dame would have known that nigga paid attention to everything about me down to the fact I didn't use pads instead tampons and the brand I preferred.

Dame's baby mom had continued to call all types of the night and demand random shit from him, but I didn't allow it to interfere with what we had going because Dame was home every night before a certain time. Kena even blew my phone up for the first week or so of us being together but I shut that shit down really quick when I changed my number on that hoe. There was no way I was about to allow her to blow my phone the fuck up whenever she felt the need for nothing, if she wanted me that bad she obviously knew where I stayed so there was nothing stopping her from bringing her tail to my place and fixing any problem she felt the need to. I won't say he is perfect but until he gives me a reason to think otherwise, I believe he is being loyal to me and what we have. He hasn't officially moved in but you would never know because he sleep here every fucking night; there isn't a night that goes by that he doesn't put me to bed or wake me up throughout the night for what he calls his pussy. I'm not complaining because just like he can't get enough of me I can't get enough of that dick either. What he had between his legs has truly turned into my newfound addiction and I'm not trying to quit it.

I made an appointment at Planned Parenthood today to confirm my assumption about me being pregnant as well set up an appointment to get an abortion. I hadn't told Dame that I thought I was pregnant, when he asked about my period, I simply told him they were irregular, and I could go sometime without having a cycle and he was coo with that answer. I hated that I had to lie to him, but I didn't want to face what he would possibly say or feel about becoming pregnant so early on in our relationship. It's not that we were doing good but I felt that it would be best if I didn't have a child this young and without stability in our future, we haven't even been together officially for six months. I refuse to be another baby mom of his and shit not work out between us. Of course, the clinic confirmed my assumption and I was indeed pregnant. I made my first payment and set the date to have the procedure completed. I didn't want to prolong the process any longer in fear of symptoms coming along or worse for me to start showing. Getting into the car I sent the girls a message in group text informing them I was pregnant and that I had set an appointment to have the pregnancy aborted. Of course, they all supported my decision rather they agreed with it or not. Renee told me she would accompany me the day of the procedure and Netia promised to help me after if I needed anything. Lee replied letting me know she was sorry she couldn't be here, but I informed her it was ok and that I knew if she could she would. I also made them all promise not to slip up and tell anyone because if word got back to Dame, I feared how things would go.

It was the day of my appointment and I can lie and say I wasn't scared shitless the most I had ever done was get a pap smear twice a year. I never had any major or minor surgeries so I was scared of how my body would react and feel after everything was said and done. Dame was off to work by the time I woke up, so I didn't have to explain to him where I was going and why Renee had to take me instead of driving myself. I made sure to fuck him good all night long because the nurse informed me at my first appointment that after the procedure that I would be bleeding and wouldn't be able to have sex for six weeks. I'm still not sure how I'm going to get Dame not to touch me for six weeks but I'm going to have to figure some shit out and quick. Pulling up to the clinic I'm sure Renee could see the look of fear and sadness in my face because she asked me was, I was ok and had I had a change of heart. I informed her my mind was made and I was just a little nervous. Grabbing our purses and heading into the clinic Renee reached for my hand and we walked hand in hand. The smallest gesture made this whole process a little easier for me to face.

After an hour and a half of the procedure and recovery it was all done and over and I felt normal once it was time to leave. The nurse gave me a prescription for birth control as well as a list of OBGYNs to follow up with if I didn't have my own but not before giving me a brown paper bag filled with condoms. I think that was their way of telling me to be more careful and not to bring my ass back here. We dropped my prescription off at the local Walgreens by my house and headed to pick up Netia so she could help me if need be. I decided I would tell Dame I didn't feel well and was cramping from a normal menstrual cycle and that Netia needed my car since I had already requested off a couple days anticipating the procedure being worse than it actually was.

While sitting around the house bored as shit Netia had fallen asleep on me and Dame was over his dads helping his father and Dupree remodel the basement so he would be here until late I took my free time to snoop and be nosy on Dame's baby moms Facebook. Dame hadn't given me any reason to doubt his loyalty to me, but yawl know us women still have to check and see for ourselves if there's some funny shit present. After checking her page, I saw she hadn't made any subliminal or post about Dame, so I was satisfied and logged off. When Dame walked into the house Netia woke up on key and grabbed her belongings and gave me a hug letting me know she would see me tomorrow. Dame didn't take anything of her taking my car and leaving because I had already sent him a text informing him of the story, we made up for her needing my car and me not feeling too well so I took off.

It had been a month since my abortion and Dame and I still hadn't had sex although the bleeding only lasted the first few days after. I was scared after but once I started my birth control pill, I was now hornier than ever and ready to fuck my man, but he hadn't made in moves or passes on me. For Dame to not want to have sex was completely out of the ordinary. The first week or so he was pissed but I always made sure to suck his dick to the point of no return and let him know it was only a period and wouldn't last forever. I didn't want for him to grow impatient, start assuming other shit or even look for a quick nut in the nest bitch so I made sure to drain his nut faithfully before he went to sleep and before he left the house. Last night I tried to get Dame to have sex with me, but he gave me some bullshit ass excuse talking about he was too tired. Yeah, he was still working, hustling, as well helping his father remodel his house but that never stopped him any other time. Shit last night he wouldn't even allow me to suck his dick, that shit raised a red flag but until the proof is brought forward, I'm just going to sit back and chill before I lose my nigga off assumptions alone.

Dame started bringing Dame the third around me last week and I was happy to know he finally felt comfortable bringing his son to meet me and spend time with us together. I wasn't ready for a child of my own, yet I enjoyed spending time with Dames son, maybe that's because I could send him right back home if and when I was tired. Today we were going to the movies to see some kid movies that I thought would be great as one of our first actual outings. Dame was resistant at first but after having to guilt trip him into us spending quality time lately he finally gave in. We had so much fun at the movies and Lil Dame enjoyed himself. We ate all types of pizza and junk food and even allowed him to have his very own bag of cotton candy from the theater. He was beyond tired by the time we reached the car. Before we were completely out of the parking garage of the movie theater, he was sound asleep. Dame dropped me off at home and headed to drop off lil Dame. I hadn't realized how sleepy I was until I woke up the next morning not even remembering drifting to sleep. Seeing that Dame's side of the bed was still made caused me to hope up and search the apartment for any signs of Dame being home or even still being here but there were none. I checked my phone to see if I had any missed calls and there were none. I immediately went into panic mode thinking the worst, I called Dame and he answered on the fourth ring right before it went to voicemail.

"What's up Bae?" Dame answer still sounding asleep.

"Bae is everything ok? I just woke up and saw you didn't make it back home last night?" I asked with fear still in my tone.

"Yeah, I'm coo, I stopped by my pops house and ended up just staying here after talking with him and having a few drinks." I let out a sigh of relief before responding to his comment. I couldn't help but to still feel some type of way because he hadn't even sent me a text letting me know where he was.

"Oh, ok well since you ok, I'll let you get back to sleep cause that's what it sounds like you were doing before I called." I stated sarcastically.

"Yep, I'll hit you up when I wake up" he said dryly. Instead of responding I ended the call and headed to the shower so I could get dressed and head into work for some over time on my day off since I didn't have anything else to do for the day.

It had been about three days since Dame stayed at my place. I know he doesn't live with me but after practically being with him every night and waking up in his arms I had become accustomed to him being there with me. Shit there wasn't a night I had to sleep alone since we had been together and now, I had only seen him for a few minutes here and there and talked to him over the phone. I hadn't asked why the sudden change because I believe if he wanted me to know he would have just told me or at least threw a few hints and he had done neither, so I let him be. I've never been the type to be all on a niggas dick anyways, so I was just going to fall back. I'm not in love with Dame but I have grown to love him and before I allow myself to be consumed into him to the point where I felt he was everything to me I need to start back living my life and enjoying time without him. I'm too young to be cooped in the house being depressed about a man and what he is doing anyways so tonight I was going out to get a breath of fresh air and to let my hair down with Netia and Renee. I didn't need to grab anything new to wear since I hadn't been out in so long there were a few items in my closets I could pop the tags and throw on.

We all rode together to Club Fire as we always do with Renee being the designated driver. When we stepped out, his car all eyes were on us even in the parking lot. To say we shut shit down whenever we stepped out is an understatement. Renee had on some skin tight fitted miss me jeans with a black shirt that had her entire back out and some knee-high black leather boots, rocking her hair bone straight with the part in the middle she was flawless as usual. Netia being the one out the bunch to pick a skirt for the night had on a brown knee length pencil skirt with a cream-colored loose-fitting sleeveless shirt and a brown leather jacket and boots to match. Netia was rocking her hair in a high ponytail that fell down to the middle of her back. I chose to rock a pair of ashy grey Rock jeans with a black halter and black leather jacket, thigh high black leather boots and my bob was slayed to the Gods with purple streaks. You could hear bitches whispering and niggas whistling as we headed for the VIP line at the door. There was no way we planned on standing in line no matter the cost. Looking as fly as we did would almost be a contraction to waiting in the normal ten dollars for a headline. As soon as we got inside, we made our way straight to the bar we all hadn't been out since the night of Dames birthday and were in need of this night. The music was rocking, and the crowd was heavy. I witness a couple boss niggas walk by and eye us as we waited to give our order for drinks. Instead of finding a spot to sit and sitting pretty we all decided tonight we would mingle and stay in the crowd just enjoying the breath of fresh air we all longed for.

Instead of my normal, I started with a double shot. I got a triple shot of Patron and headed to the dance floor "Yo Gotti DM" was playing and everyone was singing and rapping the lyric whether their DM was going down or not. I checked my phone and to my surprise I didn't have any missed calls or text from Dame, and I hadn't spoken with him all day. Even with us not seeing each other we still spoke at least once a day, but I guess today was different. Renee was drinking more than normal, and I was happy to see she was enjoying herself and not worrying about Mark or anything else. Netia was on a prowl and I could see it in her eyes. She took her double shot to the head and she was already on her second one. As the song went off I looked over to tell my girls I was about to head to the ladies' room to touch up because I was sweating my ass off and wanted to make sure I was still looking just as good as I was when I walked into the club. The ladies' room wasn't packed like I expected it to be. There were only two chicks in there one holding the door shut for her friend and the other washing her hands. The chick looked familiar, but I couldn't put my finger on where I knew her from exactly, hopefully by the end of the night I could remember. One thing about me I may not always remember names or where exactly I knew someone, but I never forgot a face. I was wiping the sweat from my face and applying a coat of my MAC gloss to my lips. I peeped ol girl eyeing me from the corner of my eye while she was waiting in the corner by the door. As soon as the bathroom stall door opened, I saw Lena's face in the mirror, and it all made sense now why the chick in the corner looked so familiar. It was the bitch that was with her the night of Dames birthday party and she was eyeing Dupree. Lena looked just as pissed to see me as I was feeling but I would never let her see that. Instead I kept putting my lip gloss on as if I hadn't even noticed her. I knew the bitch wasn't about nothing, rather I was in the restroom alone or not she knew that she didn't want these problems. Lena didn't even wash her hands with her nasty ass, she simply headed straight out the restroom without looking back. I headed out right after here and joined my girls back by the bar to get another triple shot, Lena wouldn't know but she just egged me on even more to turn up just seeing her face pissed me off because I knew Dame wasn't going a day without talking to his son so I knew she had been in contact with him today and I hadn't.

Is that her in the VIP-line
With the Vuitton and Yves saint Laurent
Used to drive the Nisan, now she in a Beamer
I don't want 'er cause she from the corner
And I heard that Beamer was a loaner
Her old man, the owner
And I don't even drink Corona's
What type of drink you want girl?
I'm Champagne forever
I'm dirty Sprite forever

Future "Turn on the light" was booming through the speakers as we made our way back to the dance floor. I started swaying my hips and not only feeling my drink but the song as well. I felt someone burning a hole in my back, so I played it off by continuing to dance while turning around. Low and behold it was Dame standing in the flesh eyeing me with his lustful eyes. As mad as I was at him, his stare was hypnotizing, my thong was drenched, and I would be needing to take another trip to the ladies' room but for a different reason this time. I turned back around and broke our eye contact so I wouldn't fall for his bullshit because I needed to stand strong and continue to enjoy my night without Dame being a part of it. Knowing that Kena and Dame were in the same facility, I had to keep my eyes open because at the end of the day we were still a couple and I would be damn if Kena tried some foul shit with my man in my presence. I gave Renee and Netia that look, and they didn't even need to ask any questions; they simply followed me to the ladies' room. Reaching the restroom, I informed them of the earlier encounter with Kena and that Dame was also in attendance tonight so that they would be in the p's and q's and keep an eye out for anything. After our miniature conference in the ladies' room we all decided to go fuck the dance floor up and show our asses. You would have thought Renee and Netia had a point to prove as well because they were going just as hard as I was like they had a nigga in the club as well. I knew that Dame would be pissed seeing me out turning up but that's exactly what his ass deserved after acting the way he had been as of lately. In all honesty I was hoping Dame sent me a text message and he would be kissing my ass, but he didn't.

Ciara's "Body party" started playing and as bad as I wanted to find my man, I knew it would be like finding a needle in the haystack so I just slowly swayed and grinded my hips to the beat alone. Some fine ass Chocolate nigga had grabbed Netia up and was slow winding with her and Renee had declined every guy who came up to her, so she too was dancing alone. I looked over to my left and spotted Kena in Dames face trying to dance on him. Although he didn't see me watching he still wasn't dismissing her fast enough for me. I got ready to head over there and Renee grabbed my wrist stopping me in my tracks. "Nah boo don't even go over there sit back and watch and see how he acts when he thinks you're not around. Keep enjoying your night, don't allow that hoe to ruin your mood." Renee stated with a slight slur to her words.

"You're right boo I'm bout to sit back and watch and if I don't like what I see then two can play that game" I said standing back and observing the two of them. I'm guessing Kena's little friend had caught my glares and informed Kena I was watching because she turned to face me and started moving her ass on Dame. Dame didn't seem to be paying Kena any attention, but he wasn't moving her off of him either pissing me off even more. When I looked up to see my eyeing him it was too late because some random Guy who I'm guessing was friend with the nigga Netia was dancing with approached me and asked to dance. Normally I would've declined out of respect for Dame but since he wanted to be disrespectful so was I. I started fucking it up to every beat in the song. I could feel this fine ass stranger's manhood growing with my every move and I can't say I was disappointed by what I felt, he was definitely blessed in that department if you ask me. I looked over and Dame had a killer stare on me and looked as if he was about to break not only my neck but the niggas as well. I simply gave him a smile, winked, and turned to face the stranger wrapping my arms around his neck and singing along with Ciara. I was getting into the song and feeling my drink when I felt Renee yank my arm "LETS GO NOW!" through gritted teeth she yelled. I didn't ask any questions I just let her lead the way and got the fuck out of dodge with Netia on my heels. I wasn't going to protest at any questions until we reached the car. No sooner than we were all seated in the car and heading out the parking lot Netia was screaming for Nae to pull over. Soon as she pulled over the car wasn't even at a complete stop Netia opened the door and started throwing up. I didn't think she was that fucked up nor had drunk that much but she was spitting out everything she had taken in the entire night. When she was done Renee hopped on the freeway, Netia and I started with the questions. "What the fuck was that back there, why did you practically drag us out of there?" I asked with Netia cosigning "yeah what was that all about?" "While yawl two was fucking on the dance floor with those two niggas Kris, Dame and Dupree had all given us looks to kill and were headed in our direction. I didn't know what the fuck was about to pop off but I know my brother and if there's a problem that causes him to give those looks I know I don't want any parts in it and neither do you two. So instead of standing around to see what the fuck was about to happen I got us out of harm's way." "I figured it was something like that, but good thing I got ol boys' number because all the sweet nothings he was whispering in my ear were sounding damn good to a bitch" Netia said causing us all to laugh. "I don't know why they were so mad, and Dame got some fucking nerve after the stunt he pulled allowing his baby mom to disrespect me and pop her nasty ass booty all over him." I said thinking about the two of them in the club only pissed me off even more. "

you right but then wasn't the time to find out, I'm going to call Kris in the morning to see what happened and I'll let yawl know soon as I find out" Renee stated as she pulled up to my place. I hoped out and staggered all the ways up the steps and laid right onto my couch as soon as I closed my front door. That Patron did a number on me and I knew I over did it cause the room was spinning.

7

DAME

know yawl like about time this nigga speaks up. Well yawl know me as Dame and that's just who I am, sike na but I'm Dame Jr, everyone used to call me DJ growing up but now the only person who I allowed to refer to me as DJ now being a grown ass man was my Pops. Dupree is my older brother and we are damn near complete opposites, even with the same mother and father. I'm the hot head of the two. I fuck shit up and ask questions later, I'm more of a lady's man and could give two fucks about one bitch when I have a whole list to replace her with. Don't get me wrong I know Erin is my woman and your probably thinking what the fuck am I talking about, but up until Erin I hadn't really been committed to a female since getting my heart broken by my first love in high school. After that shit I vowed to never give my all to one woman. Something about Erin and our connection made me want to try again but I can't say this shit was easy with so many women available at my beck and call, shit I'm trying and for now that's all I can do. If I was a bitch, I would want me too shit I'm what many would refer to as a pretty boy and I take no offense to it. I'm a skinny nigga but don't let that fool you a nigga got muscle shit I work construction with my pops part time so I can't be no weak nigga. I stand five foot nine and I'm tattooed like the subway

96

in Harlem. I keep my goatee trimmed really nice to compliment my braids at all times. So, you see there aren't many things a female won't like about a nigga like myself; I work legally and hustle even harder, my swag alone is enough to make a bitch fall in love.

I have one son and I didn't even know he existed until a few months back. Kena had accused me of getting her pregnant but she disappears when I told her it wasn't mines and that I suggest she get an abortion. She had moved out of town with her older cousin and stayed the fuck away from me until my son was damn near a year old. I hadn't told anyone about my son because I wasn't sure if he was mine until the DNA came back to prove he was indeed my son, my pops, Dupree, and Kris knew all about the situation but no one else. Kena was a jump off and I kind of hoped she wouldn't be pregnant by me but shit that happens when you take a hoe home. At twenty-three I felt my life was just beginning and I didn't have time for the baby momma drama that would come along with her and boy was I right Kena came with a whole suitcase of that shit. She was drama at its finesse and the pettiest bitch I had ever met. Kena wasn't bad on the eyes, that's the only thing that saved her ass. Kena stood about five foot five and weighed about 130. She wasn't the thickest, but she had a nice little shape on her. Kena is brown skin and puts you in the mind of Gabrielle Union. She keeps weave n so I'm not sure how long or short her real hair is, and I really don't give a fuck. Kena is an all-around party animal and you can catch her at every local club or event Thursday through Sunday kid and all, she finds a way to go out. Kena doesn't work and she shares a place with her cousin Ciara from Kentucky. The only reason she has a ride is because I couldn't go for her catching the bus with my little man in tow. But enough about her rat ass.

Shit had been sweet with Erin and I since the day I made her officially my girl, but it was causing a strain on the relationship with Kena. Not that I had any type of serious relationship with Kena, but she wasn't allowing me to get my son as often and even complained when she found out I had him around Erin. Kena and I were never anything besides a fuck, but she couldn't seem to get that through her thick ass skull. The moment she found out that I made shit official with Erin and Erin had been around my son she threatened to put me on child support knowing damn well I take good care of my seed, plus I didn't want the courts all in my personal life and business. Kena even went as far as threatening to move away with my son and I knew she would do it just because of the type of bitch she was. Shit if I would have never known about it him, I wouldn't give a fuck but since he's been in my life I refuse to not be in his or without him.

Erin that's my little boo fa real, I never knew shorty was so coo. I mean I knew she had a little crush on a nigga since she was younger but I never paid it no mind because she was younger than me, but as time passed and I got to know her she started seeming more and more like a good catch. The night of little going away party I guess Erin finally got the courage to finally make it know she was feeling a nigga and it's been downhill from there. On top of Erin being coo as shit baby is cold as fuck. There isn't a flaw about her in my eyes, she's the closest to perfect I've seen in my city. She works hard and I admire that about her, Erin's never worried about competing or being in competition with the next female no matter what it is she has a lane of her own she remains in. I can sit and politic with Erin about any and everything without shorty passing any type of judgement on me or my opinion and that makes our relationship so much stronger. Erin accepts the fact that I have a child even though she has none of her own. Just recently I started bringing my son to Erin spot for a few hours here and there just to see how she would interact with him and so far, so good, my lil man's likes shorty so that's a plus. I'm glad shorty doesn't have any children because I'm not the type to wife a bitch let alone one with a bunch of baggage because with kids comes baby daddy and that alone screams drama. I guess now that I have a child, I have to be more considering of females having kids but I'm still getting used to being a parent to my own child let alone playing step daddy to the next niggas kids.

I try to see my son on a daily basis, but like I said Kena is making it harder and harder on a nigga. My everyday visits turned into every other day which is fine by me as long as I get to talk to him daily. Our conversations are short as hell because he's only one but it's the principle of me knowing he's ok. Some nights I stay over Kena's house and lay with him until he falls asleep just so that he knows that even if I don't live with him and his momma, I'm still there for him. Kena hates the fact that after lil Dame is asleep I leave instead of just staying the night over her crib but I'm not even trying to go that route with her. As messy as Kena's ass is she's they type of bitch that would snap some pictures of a nigga in his sleep or some sneaky shit like that just to post on social media and make my girl mad. Kena be so pressed that as soon as I leave her crib, she finds a reason to start blowing my phone up and text messaging me even if it doesn't have to do with my son. I can tell that Erin grows impatient with the constant nagging of Kena at times, but she doesn't complain or express it to me. Kena talks shit when she assumes it's because of Erin. I'm not answering her calls, but I know deep down she doesn't want no problems with Erin. Erin may be a reserved type of chick but don't get it twisted baby girl will throw them hands no questions asked. I remember back in the day her, Lee, and their other friend Netia stayed beating bitches up that would step out of line with Kris, and the crazy part is they were young and still takin no shit from nobody.

A couple weeks back Erin was feeling bad having a bad ass menstrual cycle that lasted for what seemed like forever I was tempted to fuck with Kena but the night I damn near slipped up there was some funny shit going on with Kena. When Kena undressed and spread her legs I took a good look at her pussy while playing with my dick and realized some shit was definitely wrong. It looked like she had some sort of blisters or something on the inside of her pussy lips. That shit caused me to go soft as fuck in less thana matter of seconds. After looking at her shit I put my dick back in my pants and asked her what the fuck was wrong, this bitch had the nerve to tell me not to play stupid. She caught me all the way off guard when she hoped up and started going off accusing me of being the one to give her the shit, then to find out it was herpes she was accusing me of spreading really pissed me off. I knew for a fact I didn't have any sores or shit like that on my dick and there was no way I was taking the blame for no nasty shit I didn't do. I was drunk that night but not drunk enough to fuck her nasty ass after seeing that nor believe I had the shit too. I took that as a sign to keep my man in my pants and took my drunk ass home to my girl. I couldn't even touch Erin after that night I knew I was clean but until I made sure with the paperwork to prove it, I had to be careful and not take any chances. Since that night that shit had been replaying in my head and I was wondering how long Kena's nasty ass had that shit, and if she felt I was the one who gave it to her why was that the first time she ever mentioned the shit to me. Even though Erin was trying her hardest to pretend shit was normal I could tell something else was bother her but I'm not a nigga to sit down and talk about what's wrong. Like I said I'm a man of actions and talk later so if there was a problem I was going to wait until Erin felt woman enough to address the shit instead of kissing her ass to see what was wrong. I even went to two separate doctors the morning after and I had been awaiting a call back or paperwork from either doctor in the mail to confirm I was clean. I hadn't heard anything from the doctors, but I was still stressed the fuck out.

The last couple of days I had been working extra hours helping out my pops with the last little bit of remodeling on this need building we had just recently purchased for a business plan me and my brother were planning on. I hadn't told Erin the details because we wanted it to be a surprise to everyone that Dupree and I were soon to be business owners and attempting to give up the block one hundred percent. Erin was blowing me up, but I was too tired to talk or even go to her place. Since it would all be over with by the end of this weekend, I would let her know the big secret Monday morning once the final paperwork was signed. My brothers and I decided to head out to club fire and celebrate our recent accomplishment of becoming soon to be business owners, as bad as I wanted to turn up I was still fuck up awaiting confirmation from the doctors about my health.

Running into Erin was a shock she hadn't been going out often, but I figure she probably needed to let off some steam since we both had been acting really weird towards each other lately. I was pissed to have run into Kena but I knew the type of bitch Kena was so I should have expected to run into her at the club. I guess Erin saw Kena trying to twerk on a nigga and felt the need to get some get back and started showing her ass on the dance floor with some nigga. I was going to let the shit slide until Kris told me it was a cat; we had an altercation a few months back because she shorted us on some money and had been missing ever since then. At that moment I knew I was really about to hurt the nigga it was bad enough he was all up on my shorty so to have fucked with my money to he had to be handled right then and there. By the time we made our way across the club to where the niggas were at Renee, Erin and Netia had hauled ass out of the club. Needless to say, we fucked up the cat and his weak ass partner right there in the middle of the dance floor. After kicking them niggas as we headed out of the club, for some odd reason Kena must have thought since I allowed her to get away with the shit in the club that we were back on good terms so she was waiting at my car when we reached the parking lot. When I shut shorty down and told her there was no way I was EVER fucking with her again and that the next time she pulled some stupid shit like that to piss off my girl I was going smack her ass my damn self. I also told her if it wasn't about my son, she had no reason to call or even contact me and that I would be going to court my damn self to get visitation set up. My words must have pissed her off because before I knew it she was storming off telling me she would have the last laugh I knew she was up to some grimy shit because it would be too much like right if she just walked off and left me alone that easily.

When I woke up this morning, I had ten missed calls from Erin and a four-page text message from her going off. Erin had never really spazzed out on a nigga except when Kena pulled that prank with her car months back, but she was much more pissed this time and I could tell from the words in her text message she was really contemplating being done for good with a nigga. Erin said that Kena had inboxed her last night on Facebook telling her that I had herpes and gave it to her and that she needed to get tested as well. Erin told me not to worry about picking up my shit because she would be taking it to Kris parents' house and to lose her number and how much she fucking hated me. As bad as I wanted to just say fuck it, I was honestly starting to fall for shorty, and I wasn't going to allow Kena to break us up. I hopped up and went straight to the doctor's office I was checked out at. When I had the paperwork from both Doctors office stating I was clean, and all test came back negative I felt like a weight had been lifted off my fucking shoulder. The nurses in both clinics explained the reason they hadn't reached out to me was because the news was good news, but that wasn't good enough for me, I needed proof. Not only did I need the proof for myself but to show Erin as well. I knew she was believing every word Kena had said and was probably thinking my distance lately was because I was back fuck with her, but I honestly hadn't cheated with Kena or any other women for that matter. For once in my life I didn't have a reason to cheat Erin's pussy was like heaven on earth and even when I wasn't getting it the way she sucked my dick made me feel like bitch toes curling an all.

Two weeks had passed, and I still hadn't talked to Erin. She had a nigga on the block list and even changed her locks to her crib. Like she promised she had all my shit at Kris parents' house waiting on me, I was thankful she hadn't told anyone what was going on between us because they would all be looking at me like I was crazy. Thank God I had the proof that Kena was a fucking lie it's the principle of that being a niggas reputation she was fucking with. I had sent flowers, candy, edible arrangements, and all types of little shit to Erin's job and she still wasn't trying to hear a word from me. Our business was set to open up next month and I wanted to share the good news with her but with the way she was acting I was sure she wouldn't be there to celebrate our grand opening. Today was the last day I was going to accept her ignoring and pretending I never existed. I had the paperwork in hand along with a promise ring I had Renee help me pick out. I was going to explain the entire situation to her and hopefully win my shorty back. Before I could knock on her front door, I heard her singing as bad as she sounded, I could help but smile, little shit like this made me miss her even more. I had to put my pride aside and get this shit over and done with.

"Who is it?" Erin screamed

"Open up Erin I need to talk to you" I said in my most sincere voice

"For what Dame I don't have nothing to say to you! Go back and be with your burning ass baby mom, that's who you want anyways!" She yelled back through the closed door.

"Man, Erin open this fucking door and hear a nigga out! Shit I'm sick of playing this damn cat and mouse game with your ass" I yelled back matching her tone. There was no way I was giving in that easy after coming over her looking like a fucking sucker.

"Ain't nobody playing games with you Dame, I'm coo. You can go on and be a family with that bitch." Erin snapped sarcastically.

"Erin if you don't open this fucking door, I sear I'm going to kick this bitch in" I yelled as I kicked the door forcefully. I guess she must have known I meant every word I said because I could hear her unlocking the door from the other side.

"Listen Dame I really ain't in the mood for this right now so can you just please leave?" Erin's entire tone had changes and the anger she had in her voice just seconds ago was replaced with hurt and fear. I hated that I had caused her to feel this way and I planned on doing everything in my power to fix this mess.

"Erin baby just hear me out and I promise if you still want me to leave after that I will leave, but I can't promise it will be the last time you see me" I said with a smile on my face and I could see my presence was cause her to easy up some because a smile crept on her face after my last statement.

8

LEE

I thought College would be so much more difficult than what it had actually been. Honestly I think it's actually easier than high school, there's no teachers on your back and you can do shit at your own pace as long as you have it turned in by the end of due date most professors don't give two fucks how you get it done or when. On the other hand, my relationship with Coby is shit as fuck. I hate all the distance between us and I'm starting to regret coming to school so far away from home. I know if I would have just opted to attend Ohio State University things would be completely different between us. I had been really considering transferring for next year, I had even applied and completed my financial aid for next school year with hopes I would be accepted in enough time to transfer when the fall semester came around. Tonight, I'm going to my first Frat party of the year. Since I moved down here the only thing I had ever done was study, practice, play back and more studying. When I told Coby about my plans or the night of course he had a fucking fit. It's not like he didn't kick it with his friends on a nightly basis, but he didn't approve of me finally getting out to have a little bit of fun. As bad as I wanted to cancel on my roommate and stay in my dorm so Coby wouldn't be upset I had promised her once my season was over I would finally take her up on her offer and I'm a woman of my word. Since the basketball season was now over, I didn't have to worry about any early morning practice to attend. I had a good first season of college basketball. Although we didn't go to the championship we played hard. My last game my entire family made a trip up here to support me. I was happy as hell to look in the stance and see them all looking out on the court smiling at me, I was a little disappointed when I didn't see Coby but he claimed to have something come up at the last minute and couldn't make it. He promised to make it up to me over my spring break so that's what I looked forward to.

This party was unlike any high school party I had ever been to although it was in a house it was far from your average house party. There were Frat guys everywhere and they were scrolling all up and through this house. I thought that shit was so sexy I made me want to join a women's fraternity but not her maybe once I transfer to Ohio State. Kelly knew damn near every nigga that walked past us and I blamed that on her many night of partying instead of studying. If the saying "it's not about what you know it's who you know" was true, Kelly would definitely be ok with her in West Virginia because she was far from lame around here. Kelly had given me two cups of this blue "Jungle juice" and I swear it was the tastiest shit I had ever had. After the third cup I can say I'm beyond drunk and it's time for me to report back to my dorm but of course Kelly isn't ready to leave. It's well after club hours and this party's still jumping, I don't know how these people do it. Coby had been blowing my phone up for the last hour and I didn't want to answer because there wouldn't be any way he could hear me any how and that would only piss him off even more. The crowd was finally starting to clear out and Kelly's hot ass had disappeared upstairs somewhere. I took a seat on a chair in the corner of the room and waited for her to return since I rode with her. I was scrolling through my Facebook trying to keep my drunken eyes focused when I felt someone sit down in the chair next to mine and bumping my leg slightly.

"My fault sweety" the stranger apologized

"You good," I said, not taking my eyes off my phone.

"What's your name sweety I haven't seen you around here before and why you sitting over here by yourself?" I looked up and was shocked to see the sexiest nigga I had ever seen in my entire like. His appearance caught me off guard. I was speechless and I'm guessing he could tell I was stuck in my own thoughts because he spoke up.

"You alright baby girl?" he asked with a slight smile on his face.

"I'm sorry I'm just a little drunk, but my name is Lee. I normally don't go out much so that explains why you've never seen me around. I'm here with my roommate but she don' up and disappeared on me" I finally found the words to answer all of his questions but was still taken away by his entire presence.

"I'm Rodney but everyone calls me Rod for short. I don't go out much myself if it isn't with my Frat brothers."

"Oh, so you're a part of this fraternity?" I asked slightly impressed

"Yeah, I'm actually in this house, this my last year living here though. I graduated last year but chose to stay another year on campus before moving."

"Wow must be nice, I'm in my freshmen year but I'm not too sure about continuing here. I'm still a little unsure."

"Damn I would've never taken you for a freshman, most freshmen are wild, and it shows that college is their first breath of freedom. You carry yourself well Lee. I like that!"

Since the night at that Frat Party Rod and I had been talking on the phone, texting, and even went to dinner a couple of times. He is super coo and easy to talk to. Whenever I was in need of help finishing up any homework or assignments that may have required a study partner, he took the time out of his schedule to assist me. The thing I liked about Rod was he never made any moves or tried to push up on me like most upperclassmen did with freshmen. Rod respected me and the fact that I had a whole relationship back at home. He didn't have any girlfriend, but he was honest about the fact that there were a couple of females that he kicked it with. I would be a fool to think any different. Rod let me know that he wasn't looking to push me into anything he just enjoyed my company and the friendship that we were building and I was ok with that, I had never had a male best friend and he was becoming that in such a short period of time. Rod is about five foot eleven inches tall weighing about one hundred and eighty pounds. His body was the perfect sight and the fact that he worked out often was very evident. I'm normally not into light skin guys but he was beautiful. Being Filipino and black he was blessed with the prettiest jet-black hair that he kept in a low cut. His dimple in his left cheek complimented the perfect smile he had.

There were many nights I would be upset with the way things were going with Coby and I and Rod were always there with great words of advice and never judged me for still wanting to be with Coby. I talked with Rob just as much as I did my girls back home. I could tell that Kelly didn't like how close I had gotten with Rod because of her side comments about him being a male whore or the fact that he was known for fucking freshmen bitches and leaving them looking stupid; I hadn't told her the relationship that we shared I only allowed her to assume and make an ass out of herself. Beside it was none of her damn business anyways. I had lived with her damn near a whole year and she had fucked more niggas than me and all my girls put together, so she had no room to call anyone a whore rather it was true or not. I couldn't care less about who all Rod fucked with because I didn't look at him like that, we were friends nothing more nothing less and I respected his privacy when it comes to the females he talks to. Rod told me one night Kelly tried to get at him and he had turned her down, but what I found funny about the situation was that she waited until after he and I became friends to ever make a move when she knew him as well all his Frat brother way before I even knew he existed. Kelly never mentioned it to me, so I never told her I knew anything about it. Rod had called me this morning telling me that Kelly came at him today in the student union talking shit about me and Coby, now for what reason I don't know but I guess that was her way of throwing shade. Little did this hoe know I talk to Rod about Coby and I and he knows how I feel about my relationship, it wasn't her place to even run and tell what she overheard me arguing with Coby about either way so as soon as she walks in this room I have all intentions of letting her ass have it. Rod told me not to let it bother me and not to sweat it but I told him if I allowed her this one pass she would only continue and think it was ok to run my business to the next person and I don't do that messy shit. It was bad enough I was tied as hell from staying up all night studying for my finals before I leave for spring break but the argument I had with Coby last night had me feeling some type of way so Kelly was for sure about to feel my wrath.

Kelly walked into the room like shit was sweet and greeted me as normal. I couldn't even fake the funk before I knew It, I was up off my bunk and in her face.

"Look bitch I'm going to tell you this only one time and I'm not gonna say shit else the next time I'm going simply slap the shit out of your messy ass! What the fuck I talk about on the phone with my fucking boyfriend all the way in Columbus is none of your fucking business nor your place to run and tell the next nigga. I don't give a fuck what you heard or what you think you know keep my fucking name out your nasty ass mouth. Flat the fuck out!"

"Wait first off Bitch back the fuck up out my face! Secondly ain't nobody worried about your ass or your lame ass boyfriend back home. I know Rod came calling you talking shit but trust you're not even that tight to be worried about bringing your name up on the regular so you can keep all that rah rah you talking to your fuckin self."

Before I could calm myself down, I had punched the bitch straight in her shit and kept swinging fucking her ass up. It didn't matter that Kelly was bigger than me I was laying hands on this bitch and she wasn't keeping up for shit every punch she threw back in return was being returned with three more in return. It had been a minute since I had to whoop a hoes ass, so I was letting all my inner frustration out on her fucking face. She kept yelling for me to get the fuck off of her but once we fell back into the closet, I climbed on top of her and rained blows on her face back to back. She tried grabbing for my hair but mishit was too short for her to have her way like she thought she would. We didn't stop fighting until some white guys came into our room and grabbed me off of her. I was so pissed when she first walked in, I hadn't even realized we were fighting with our door wide open. No sooner than that grabbed me off the top of her she stormed out the room without saying a word. Face all fucked up and all. Since I was already done packing and ready to hit the road I grabbed my few bags and headed home for the spring break leaving our dorm room fucked up and all she could clean that shit up when she returned because I sure wasn't about to. I needed a break from West Virginia and her hoe ass.

My first stop was to see my boyfriend, we needed to make up and I needed to just be in his presence at the time. Coby was at his apartment waiting for me when I got there. As soon as I walked into his front door, he was awaiting my arrival on the couch ass naked. I can't say I minded seeing him this way because I was beyond backed up and needed to feel him inside of me. I dropped my bag and started undressing as I walked over to him. I straddled his lap without any foreplay and started kissing him as if it had been years since the last time, I saw him instead of months. Sliding down onto Coby's dick I had to take it slow, no matter how wet my pussy was I had to get back used to something this big being inside of me since it had been so long. I slowly rode his dick as he helped guide me with his strong hand on my little waist. I felt myself-getting ready to reach my climax and started working my hips even faster. Coby leaned up and took my left breast into his mouth hungrily and massaged my right with his free hand. The penetration he was giving me with a relaxing feeling he was delivering my breast with his tongue caused me to erupt on his dick as if I had just pissed on him. Cody let my breast loose and started slamming me down on his dick faster than I could handle and before I knew it he lifted me off and his nut was oozing out as he laid his head back onto the couch.

After the first day in the apartment with Coby making up for lost time fucking all day and night, I hadn't spent much time with him. Yet I was still cooped up in his place for most of my spring break. Besides stopping over my parents for a few hours here and there I hadn't done much. I haven't even spent any time with my girls, but Coby was out with his friends all day every day. Whenever I would tell him I was leaving he promised to be on his way and have an attitude as if I messed up his day. We were having the normal Sunday dinner at my parents' house. I was so happy to see everyone in attendance from Renee, Sanai. Kris, Erin, Dame, Netia, and Dupree felt like old times all over again. If it was one thing, I missed about being home, it was being in the presence of them. Cody came up with some bogus ass excuse as to why he couldn't make it, but I was so happy to be in the presents of my family that I didn't even let it affect me. After dinner I was heading back to school so if he chose to spend time elsewhere that was his loss. Over the weeklong spring break Rod and I kept in contact and I had honestly missed his company. I could talk with him as much as I would like to because he was extremely busy, but I still had to talk to him more than I had Coby and we were three hours apart. Kelly had even text me apologizing and stating that she wanted to remain friends. I told her I wasn't stressing it and that there was no hard feeling. I was being honest I really wasn't sweating it, the ass whopping I put on her was enough to prove I wasn't playing. I'm not the type to hold grudges anyhow so I was glad she knew I meant every word I said and the last month and a half of us living together wouldn't be no bullshit because if there was I wouldn't hesitate to kick her ass for the second time around.

I stopped by Coby's to grab the rest of my things before getting on the freeway and drop off the cake that my mom had made for him. Coby loved Chocolate cake and my mom made him a cake specifically for him. He's lucky I hate chocolate cake, or I would've taken half of the shit for myself back to school. Surprisingly, he was home, when I walked into the bedroom, he was sitting on the edge of his bed looking pissed off. I didn't want for us to have an argument before I went back to school so I sat beside him and tried to figure out what the problem was.

"What's up babe? You ok?" I ask while rubbing his back.

"Yeah Lee, who is Rodney?" he asked catching me of guard

"Rodney who?" I asked really confused as to who he was talking about.

"Don't play me stupid, from his Facebook information it says he goes to school with you. So, tell me who he is and are you fucking him?" I stopped rubbing his back and looked at him with confusion and frustration all over my face. I couldn't believe he really thought I was fucking someone else, especially Rod. Shit I really didn't know who he was talking about when he referred to him as Rodney because no one ever called him that.

"No Coby, why the hell would you ask me some shit like that?" I asked standing up from the bed and going to grab my bags from his closet. Before I could grab both bag Coby and walked over to me and smacked me so hard across the side of my face it caused me to stumble back into the wall. I couldn't believe he just hauled off and smacked me. I didn't know whether to fight his big ass back or just get mishit and leave I was so hurt.

"So, you really were goin play like you didn't know who the nigga was at first? Listen Lee I love you and I refuse to be here in Columbus while you parade around West V. like some little young THOT!"

"Coby, I have never and will never cheat on you. You called him Rodney and I honestly didn't know who you were talking about because none ever calls him that. He's nothing to me he knows I'm with you and he has a girlfriend I can assure you there is nothing going on between the two of us!" I said with tears streaming down my face. I couldn't believe Coby would think so low of me. He was my first and is the only guy I had ever been intimate with. Rod and I were strictly friends and there was no lie to anything told Coby about things between me and Rob.

"Ok Lee! Don't let me find out any different. I love you and have a safe trip back. Make sure you text me as soon as you make it to your dorms." Coby said before kissing me on the lips and heading out. As bad as I wanted to stick around and fix whatever was going wrong between Coby and I, I couldn't. I had to get back on the road before it was too late. Mondays are my early days and with this being my last semester before summer vacation I had to be on top of my work.

The entire ride back to school I couldn't do anything besides cry. Listening to Ciara "Sorry" wasn't helping any either. After thinking about everything that had been going on and my relationship with

Coby, I fault myself. If it wasn't for me moving away to college, we would still be just fine. Then the fact that I allowed Rod to post a picture on my wall we had taken one evening while he was helping me study as his woman crush was just stupid. Even though he didn't say anything out the way on the post I guess Coby was offended that another guy would even post me. I should've deleted the post after he tagged me in it, but I honestly didn't see any wrong in it until Coby got upset about it. If I would have known, it would cause Coby to think less when it comes to my loyalty to him, I would have never told Rod it would be ok to post any picture of me. Trust and believe as soon as I left Coby's place, I sent Rod a text message telling him to delete the picture and me from his friend list on Facebook as well Instagram because it was causing problems in my relationship. Being the gentleman Rod is, he simply apologized and did as I requested, I told him I would call him later to explain but I knew I wouldn't be telling him the whole truth.

9

COBY

f I would have known that my freshmen year would be the only year of college I completed, I would have never wasted my time and money. This school year is damn near over and I haven't made any progress in the field or with my grades. Shit if you ask me school is more of a burden than anything else going on in my life right now. To keep it all the way one hundred after I was put on probation and couldn't play football I had given up on my studies, but the reason I was put on probation was because of my grade so it's just an continuing circle of stupidity. Right after I was put on probation wasn't required to attend as many practices and my weight began to drop. I could go for my reputation to suffer along with my everything else, so I started taking steroids to keep my weight up. Those mother-fuckas are making me into a monsta. I'm walking around looking way better than before the ladies on campus are even calling me Hulk. I thought I would lose my touch once I wasn't playing, but I haven't and I'm happy to say that, I drink a lot more now too since I have more free time. I spend so much time on campus at local bars and clubs it's ridiculous. If I could spend as much time studying or in class as I do at somebody's bar, I would be passing my courses. I enjoy the effects of the steroids but the mixture of those and alcohol cause my mood swings to change drastically. My parents started noticing changes in me and have cut me off for the time being. They don't know the truth behind me not playing football or my grades but that did inform me until I was back on the field and doing things right, they wouldn't be financially helping me any longer. I had enough money saved for now so I'm ok with them not helping me out for now. I'll be back on the field by next year when the coach realizes that they need me more than I need them.

"Shit keep doing it just like that! Baby don't stop this shit feels so good" Nicole took me out of my daydream ducking my dick like a pro.

"Damn baby don't forget the balls show them some love too while you down there" I had to make sure I got the entire royal treatment instead of half because this head was for sure the best I had ever received. Every time Nicole gave me head, I was memorized like a newfound man losing his virginity. "Oh, I'm bout to nut, get up, let me feel you" I demanded, and Nicole already knew what that meant. Getting up and bending over touching the floor I rammed my hard dick inside causing Nicole to scream out.

"Yess big daddy fuck this ass like you miss it. I miss big daddy! Fuck me harder!" Nicole was certified freak on another level, and I loved that shit. I did shit I had never ever dreamed with Nicole and every time was like I was learning something new. I had never fucked any female in the ass, but I can now say I enjoy that shit way more. The ass is so much wetter than the pussy and not many can handle it, but Nicole takes the dick well.

"Shit I'm bout to cum baby! Throw that shit back for big daddy" just as I demanded Nicole did and I was letting all my nut fill the side of that ass. Nicole is sexy as fuck and different from Lee in so many ways. Nicole is pretty tall standing five-foot eleven weighting about one hundred and fifty pounds. Nicole wears those long as Brazilian bundles curls all wild and shit. Nicole had high cheekbones and the cutest smile. Body wise Lee body is way colder than Nicole's, but I can accept that Nicole had NO titties whatsoever but he ass is ok, but I'm sure that comes from taking the dick so well.

Nicole and I met at a bar on Campus around Christmas time and have been kicking it ever since. We were both drunk and fucked the first night and have been fucking like jack rabbits wherever, whenever we could. Nicole is the reason I couldn't spend as much time with Lee while she was home on spring break when I'm away from Nicole I crave that ass even when I shouldn't. The relationship I have with Nicole is so close to being perfect we have a bond that is almost like dating myself. We are alike in many ways. Nicole's family is super cool and accepts me with open arms, I have taken Nicole to meet my parents just because I haven't been on the best of terms with my parents as of lately. Nicole is a couple years older than and is more mature than Lee so that's why I think we are more compatible. I love Lee and never had intentions on things being this way between us but when I was put on probation from the team, I started realizing how different Lee and I were. Lees main focus is school and basketball and right now my focus is living my life and enjoying being Coby. Lee still has a lot of growing up to do I feel she still lets her parents dictate too much of her life and I'm not on that shit any longer with my parents and I don't think she should be either. Nicole knows all about my steroid and drinking habit unlike Lee but never passes judgement, Nicole has habits as well but those include snorting powder and drinking. I never say a word because no habit is worse than the other in my opinion. Shit a drug is a drug as long as neither of us get strung out to the point we have nothing I'm ok with it.

I think it's crazy how Lee used to be my everything I used to see myself marrying her and having children with her but not any longer. Don't get me wrong I still love her and don't want to lose her. I just feel she has a lot of soul searching to do and needs to find herself instead of being the person everyone else wants her to be. Lee also seems to be way clingier than she has ever been. I don't know if it's Nicole being in the picture that makes me feel this way or has, she always has been like this. I don't think I would have ever even backed away from Lee if she wouldn't have moved away and stayed gone. I thought she would come home more often and when she didn't it gave me too much alone time. I had put my hands on her a few times lately and it was always her fault for doing something or saying something stupid when I wasn't in the mood for the bullshit. She even talks to males and shit now claiming to only be friends with them. I'm no dummy I know no nigga has intention on being only friends with a female without intentions to fuck. When I saw some nigga name Rodney posting her as his Woman Crush my blood was boiling, I probably would have smacked her ass two more times if the first one would not have been so powerful. Since our sex life was no longer the same it wasn't much I could prove because it was me who was wasn't into it like I used to be. I only wanted Lee to suck my dick, even though Lee still basically had virgin tight pussy I just didn't want it. I had trained Lee to suck dick so well she was in the level of super head and didn't even know it. I would have her watch pornos while sucking my dick and compete with them. One-night Lee gave me 14 rounds of straight head, that's 14 nuts back to back of nothing but head. To say she wasn't trained well would be telling a damn lie, but I'm proud to say I'm the only one who can brag about feeling that shit.

I left out of my place to pick up Nicole from work after the altercation with Lee. I felt a little guilty when I got back and realized that I had a nice two-layer German Chocolate cake on the counter that her mom had sent over for me. I forgot all about asking her to make me a cake the last time I was over there with Lee. I cut a big piece of cake and ate that shit in a few bites. Lees mom was no stranger when it came to the kitchen and I was thankful she hadn't forgotten about me. By the time I was done eating my cake Nicole was sucking my dick like a vacuum cleaner. I swear the skin of my dick was ready to come off from the suction of those jaws. As I was about to nut, I felt my stomach start to rumble and I knew Nicole was powerful but damn I was getting knots in my stomach, this shit is crazy. Like always instead of nutting in Nicole's mouth I rather fuck first before I let my load off. I flipped Nicole on all fours and got down on the floor on knees and inserted my dick. Fuckin doggy style had become my favor position I see how dogs got stuck that shit felt amazing. As I was pumping in and out of Nicole's ass I felt like I had to fart and I didn't want to let that shit go and ruin the mood because I had Chinese food earlier so I knew that shit would stink. When Nicole started throwing it back my entire body relaxed. I felt a fart getting ready to escape and I could hold it. When I felt a warm feeling between my thighs, I assumed Nicole was cumming until I looked down and farted again. Looking down I saw runny dark brown diarrhea seeping down my legs. I was shitting on myself and it was flowing out freely. I pulled out my dick so fast and tried running up the stairs while holding my ass, but the shit wouldn't stop. Running to the bathroom on the second floor of my apartment I left a trail of shit behind me. This had to be the most embarrassing shit ever in life. "What the fuck Coby? Did you just shit on yourself while fucking me?" I heard Nicole yell from downstairs I couldn't even respond. I was holding onto the toilet, gripping both sides, shitting like a waterfall. I shitted so much my asshole was burning and felt raw. Every time I thought it was safe to get off the toilet it started back again.

10

RENEE

Getting things perfect for my baby girl's first birthday party had been the only thing I could focus on for weeks. I wanted to make sure it was nothing less than perfect for my baby. Sanai loved Minnie Mouse so of course that was the theme. Everything was hot pink and black with Minnie Mouse decorations everywhere. We even had someone dress up in a Minnie and Mickey Mouse costume for the kids to take pictures with the characters in a decorated little photo booth. Since we grew up on the Northside of Columbus Feddersen Recreation center ended up being the perfect size to host her party. We had more than enough space for all one hundred guests we invited. There was a sweets table set up with every candy you could imagine: all Pink, white and black matching her theme with a four tier Minnie mouse cake surrounded with miniature Minnie mouse head cake pops. The gift table turned out being three tables instead of one we had designated for her items. Everyone showed her so much love, I was so appreciative of everything she received. I didn't have to buy another thing if I didn't want to until next year's Christmas. For the kids we had a Nae Nae contest and lil Dame, Dames son killed it with his little cute self. I was happy that Dame brought him and even happier to see him and Erin and worked things out and put that shit Kena started behind him. Erin appeared to be happy with Dame and his son in her life. Although Dame bringing lil Dame was a shock to the entire family we all accepted him with open arms as if he had been around more instead of this being the first family functions he had attended.

At first, I was a little caught off guard with Mark bringing a guest especially since it was a female, nut since we were not together, I had to accept the fact that he chose to move on. I won't lie and say the girl was pretty as fuck, but she gave me a bad vibe. Mark's little girl friend had a nice shape too to be a little Asian chick, she had a little pudge I didn't know if it was just fat or a beer belly, but it looked funny on her little height. Something about the girl was off, and I think Sanai picked up on it as well because she wasn't fucking with the girl and Sanai is a friendly baby so for her to not want anything to do with the girl confirmed my suspicions. Mark had never mentioned taking Sanai around anyone other than his mom but from the way the girl was trying to reach for and talk to my daughter told me this wasn't her first time around her. I'm ok with Mark having his girlfriend around my baby if he trusts her enough to be around Sanai so did I until she gave me a reason not to.

The night after the party I found myself looking over the picture on my phone and getting a little jealous when I came across the picture of Mark, his new girlfriend, and Sanai. No one knew that I would still occasionally fucked Mark from time to time when I got horny. I tried to convince myself that it was ok since Dupree hadn't been fucking with me after giving his ultimatum, but I knew it wasn't right. Not messing around with Dupree only drove me back to fucking with Mark because I didn't have the time or patience to go out and find someone new. Now don't get me wrong I'm happy Mark has a woman because he doesn't really bother me as much as he used to and we seem to be getting along better now, it just made me feel some type of way with everyone around me being in happy relationships besides myself. Sanai went with Mark after her party and I was glad because I needed time to put away all of the gifts she received and get some well needed rest. Since Sanai started walking it was almost impossible to get anything done because she was always into everything.

My mom called me telling me to meet her at Children's hospital because Sanai was sick. Mark dropped Sani off to my parents this morning because they wanted to take her out to eat. IT was almost like a family tradition for my parents to take us out to eat for our birthdays or for my mom to cook a meal of our choice on our birthday. I was pissed that my baby had to be in Children's hospital on her actual birthday, but I knew it had to be something serious for my mother to take her when she was the queen of remedies. Getting to the hospital I was informed that they were already in the process of running tests on her and she had continuously been throwing up since Mark dropped her off. My mom said that when she was vomiting at her house, she thought she saw traces of blood and that was the reason for her bringing her into the hospital in the first place. When the doctors came back and told us that my baby was severely dehydrated from throwing up so much and being so small along with needing a blood transfusion it crushed me. There's nothing like seeing your child in pain or going through something and there's nothing you could do about it. While sitting in Sanai's hospital room waiting for the doctors to come back and tell me if I was a match to donate my baby blood, I couldn't help but pray and cry out to God to help my daughter. Mark was in the waiting room looking dumbfounded and had no explanation as to why my baby was so sick. I felt he owed me some sort of explanation because she was fine just yesterday at her party. My dad kept saying to calm down and that it could have been a virus that she caught from one of the many kids at her party and for Mark's sake he better hope that was just it. The doctors came back and informed me that Sanai had a rare blood type and I wasn't a match. I walked into the waiting area feeling defeated but was comforted seeing my entire family there to support us. Kris, Dupree, and Dame had just walked in as I was taking a seat and telling Mark she needed to get his blood test in hopes his would match hers. After waiting about thirty more minutes the doctors came back and informed us that Mark wasn't a match either. The doctor also stated that she was diagnosed with sickle cell and the hospital could give her a transfusion with blood that they had but that was my last option and resort, so I had no choice but to accept it.

Finding out that Sanai had sickle cell and neither Mark nor myself had the traits only makes me think about the fact that Mark may have not been her father. I had doubts some days but I always pushed it to the back of my mind. I'm hurt knowing that my baby has to go through life with this illness but I'm even more confused as to what I have gotten myself into. I had been keeping Sanai away from Mark as well limiting him taking her with him, not because of her being sick but because of the fact that he isn't her father. There's no way her having a rare blood type and neither of us being a match didn't prove that to me. I had Sanai so I knew for a fact that she belongs to me, but I can't say the same for Mark. Mark had been becoming more and more frustrated with his limited time with Sanai and it was only a matter of time before I could take any more of his shit. Just as I was sitting on the couch thinking about the last crazy ass text, he sent me. I heard a loud knock on the door. Rushing to answer the door before whoever it was, woke my baby up, I didn't even look out the peephole and opened the door to only be faced with Mark's evil glare.

Mark wasted no time pushing past me and slamming my front door shut. Before I could say anything, he reached back and backhanded me in my face. I reached up to grab my face and he landed another smack on the opposite side of my face. Tears begin to pour down my face and I wasn't in any type of mood or positon to fight this big ass nigga back. When Mark saw the look on my face, he reached over to grab me, and I flinched out of fear that he would hit me again. I don't know why every time he put his hands on me, I swear it will never happen again. Instead of him hitting me again like I fear it's almost like his entire mood changes as he starts caressing my face and apologizing for outing his hand on me yet again. I didn't say a word until he reached to pull up the long tee shirt I had on. I didn't have on anything besides a pair of boy shorts and my tee shirt because I was lounging around the house not expecting company.

"Mark stop! Please leave!" I said with begging eyes I wasn't in any type of mood to fuck him after he just slapped the dog shutout of me twice nor more than two minutes ago.

"Renee, I love you baby and I'm sorry please forgive me" Mark whispered while he tugged at my panties. Normally I would have been turned on considering I hadn't had any dick, but I was completely turned off by his actions.

"No, Mark I don't want to do this! Please just leave, Please!" I had asked him once again but my please fell on deaf ears. Pushing me back, Mark began to force himself on top of me one I fell back onto the couch. Tears continued to fall because the look in Mark's eyes was one I had never seen before. He was in fact a deranged as nigga but the look he was giving me now proved he was gone. The Mark I once loved no longer exists and the monster he had become was scaring the shit out of me.

"Renee this is my pussy and I don't even know why you trying to fight it, stop playing with me and trying to make this shit harder than what it has to be. You know you want this" Mark stated before whipping his dick from behind his loose-fitting sweatpants in one swift motion.

"No Mark please don't do this; Sanai is right upstairs! Please don't do this!" I was practically begging him, and he must have been tired of hearing my mouth because he covered my mouth with his left hand and guided his dick into me forcefully with his right hand. As dry as I was the pain felt like he was ripping my inside. Laying on my couch silently crying while the man who I once loved with all of me rapped me. I felt so worthless and dirty. I couldn't believe he would do something like this to me period let alone with my daughter being upstairs. I zoned out and laid there until Mark was finished. Thankfully, I had started taking birth control because he let all of his bastard seeds inside of me. When he was done, he gave me a smirk said thank you and walked out as if I had just given my body to him instead of him taking it.

As soon as Mark closed my front door, I hopped up, locked the door and ran to the shower to scrubbed any traces of him and what he had just done to me off of my skin. Getting out the shower I dried off and placed on a onesie night outfit before calling Dupree and asking him to come over. There was so much I needed to get off my chest and there was no better time than now. I was happy that he answered and thankful that he agreed to come over right away. I was finally about to confess to him the truth of Sanai being his daughter and explain to him what had just happened between mark and me.

11

DUPREE

*H*earing all the shit Mark had been putting Renee though made me want to body that nigga and I can't even lie. All I could see was red, but I had to think things out, finding out that there was a strong possibility that Sanai was mine had fucked my head up even more. I was so pissed I couldn't even stay and comfort Renee like I would have liked to. I'm more hurt than mad that I had been in Sanai's life as if she was my niece all this time and here it is, she could be my fucking daughter. Renee was going through enough, so I wasn't going to basher for the bullshit of keeping this secret away from me. As soon as I got to my car, I called Kris and Dame and filled them both in on what I just found out but left out the part about Sanai. Kris was ready to body the nigga Mark for the shit he had done to his little sister and I couldn't blame him, but we had to make our next move our best move.

Renee asked me to meet her down at the Child support office the next morning to get a DNA test. When she told me where to meet her I thought she was crazy at first, like how the fuck you going put a nigga on child's support and I don't even know if she's mines yet, but when I found out this is where the DNA test are done I felt a little silly. I couldn't help but laugh at my damn self. After sleeping

124

on everything I made my mind up that the next time I ran into the punk ass nigga Mark I was fucking him up on sight I don't give a fuck where we are at and who's around he deserves it and it's coming to him sooner or later. I don't want to risk the fact of going to jail for killing him and not be in my daughter's life. Deep down after looking at Sanai and hearing about her rare bold type I knew she was mine. Nobody knew but not only did I, but Dame as well had the sickle cell trait. I told Renee that I once the test confirms she was mines we were changing her last name as soon as possible and I would personally let the nigga Mark know his services were no longer needed.

Lately I had been spending a lot of time with Alisha; the girl I met that night at Dame birthday party at the club. It felt good to finally allow myself to get close with someone other than Renee, shit up until finding out about Sanai. I had been doing a damn good job at keeping my distance from her. Now not only was my mind all fucked but my heart because Sanai is 99.99 percent my daughter. Alisha is a wonderful woman; she is such a good person and I don't want things to go bad between us now. Alisha looks just like Nia Long. Short cut and all. Alisha seems to be everything I need she levels a nigga out. She has two sides though the side that I met at the club is like her alter ego or something because I swear, I only see that side of her once she gets liquor in her system. If you asked me everything about Alisha is coo other than the fact that she has children of her own already. There's nothing wrong with a woman having children but she has three different children by two different cats. Neither one of her baby dads are involved in her kids' lives so I don't have to worry about them but it's the principle that she just found out she may be pregnant by me. I would have been happy as hell if I found this out a week ago but now, I was feeling all types of ways there was no way I wanted two different baby moms. I always wanted to be married and live happily ever after with the mother of my children. I can't deal with the type of baby mom drama my brother experiences. I'm not ashamed of my daughter but I can't seem to find the word to break the news to Alisha that Renee and I once had something going on. As far as Alisha knows Renee is like a younger sister to me. Well shit that's as far as anyone knows.

Renee and I decided that we would break the news to everyone about everything at the same time with our families as a whole. Renee had her mom cook up a big dinner and we were all meeting at her parents' house tonight. My pops was invited to come over as well. The only two people who were going to be in attendance were Lee and Mark. Once everyone was seated at the table and grace was said Renee broke the silence and came out straight forward telling everyone everything. There wasn't a part she skipped over or left out. I was nervous but glad that she got it all out and over with so there wouldn't be any further questions. Our parents both seem to have already known my pops nor either of Renee's parents were shocked or showed any type of reaction that they didn't already know the crazy news that was just broken to them. Dames stupid ass busted out laughing as if somebody had just told a fucking joke. Kris on the other hand was pissed he removed himself from the table and headed out back to smoke. I knew he felt like he betrayed him or played him by keeping a secret like this from him, but I knew Kris and I knew he would react like this. That's exactly why I waited this long to tell him about Renee and I messed around all this time. Shit I never in a million years though I would have to break the news that his niece was my daughter. No sooner than Kris stepped out the back-patio door we heard the doorbell chime. We all looked around at each other confused on who it could've been since everyone we were expecting to come was already here. When Renee's dad came back into the dining room after opening the door, we were expecting to see the nigga Mark walk in behind Mr. Larry. The looks on all of our faces were all looks of either confusion, anger, surprise, or disbelief. I myself was pissed he felt the need to even show his face after the shit Renee shared with me. I know I said I would fuck him up on sight, but I could allow my anger to take control and disrespect Mrs. Yolanda, Mr. Larry, my pops, and most importantly my baby girl like that.

Of course, when Kris walked in a saw Mark in his parents' house all the respect flew out the window, but just know that nigga was handled. I took Renee and my daughter home when right before things got too heated. Renee explained to me that she wanted to be with me and try to make us work not only for the sake of our daughter, but she was done hiding her feelings and fighting how she felt. Deep down I wanted to try with her for those very same reasons, but I didn't want to hurt Alisha. I still hadn't told Renee about the fact that Alisha was pregnant or how serious I had gotten with Alisha. My only response to Renee was that we needed time to think about everything and we would talk about this this weekend over dinner.

Since I promised Renee, we would discuss this coming weekend, I needed to talk to Alisha quickly. Instead of talking to Alisha like the man I know I should have been I sent her a text. There was no way I could face her and see the hurt in her eyes. Alisha had started telling a nigga she loved him months back and no I hadn't said it back, but I did care about her feelings.

ME: Lisha baby I know this isn't the best way to come at you, but I need to let you know first before someone else does. I have a one-year-old daughter that I just found out is mine. I'm sorry you had to find out this way but I'm just finding out myself.

Alisha: Why the fuck would you text me some shit like that Dupree, if you're just finding out how can I get mad at you about something you knew nothing about?

ME: Because although I haven't lied to you, I haven't been one hundred percent honest with you either. My daughter is Sanai, Renee's daughter.

Alisha: What you have to be kidding me. Renee as in your best friend Kris little sister? That's some sick shit! I can't believe you! I'm so fuckin embarrassed you a had me all in that girl's face when at one-point yawl were fucking!

ME: No, I'm not kidding you and yes Renee Kris sister. Look I don't expect you to be accepting of it nor ok with it, but I had to tell you the truth. Even if you don't believe me, just know I wasn't messing around with you when I messed with her.

Alisha: Fuck you Dupree, I can't wait until I have this baby and get a DNA, I hope you're not the father!

Alisha's last text through me all the way off I'm glad I hadn't fallen for her because she wasn't completely honest with me either and I would've been pissed to find out after going through her entire pregnancy thinking the baby was mine when all alone it was only a possibility. What she didn't know is she made it even easier for me to make my decision when it came to Renee and I. Instead of texting Alisha back I sent Renee a text telling her I was on my way over.

Renee opened the door and the look on her face showed me that she was nervous to see why I had just randomly popped up to see her. I grabbed her face and started kissing her like I had never before. Of all the times Renee and I have ever been together or done anything it was always in secrecy, but now that it was all out our tension was different. Renee opened her mouth and welcomed my tongue. We were both panting and gasping for air in between our kissing. "I love you Renee and I'm going to make this thing work between us not only for my daughter but for you as well, trust me you will never hurt again." I told her meaning every word that came out of my mouth. "I love you too Dupree" She said as I felt a tear on my cheek as it slid down her face. If it wasn't tears of joy, I made a promise to myself that this would be the last tear Renee shed if I had any control over it.

12

LEE

I had been anticipating this day for the past month or so. It was finally the last day I would see this place hopefully ever, but I was still unsure since I hadn't received my letter of acceptance for Fall semester at Ohio State University. Summer break is something I looked forward to, there was no way in hell I planned on taking any summer course I needed a break from class, test, and homework. Ending my freshman year with straight "A" and landing on the dean's list I'm more than proud of myself. I had already packed all of my belongings that I would be taking back home with me over the past week and it was now time for me to hit the road. It was a bittersweet feeling to be actually leaving West Virginia. Rod and I had become so close, and I was going to miss him so much over this break, but he promised to come visit me once he was done with his two-week internship for the city he had landed. On the other hand, I was happy as hell to be leaving Kelly. Yeah, I dropped the problem we had before spring break, but I still didn't like living with her snake ass. After that one incident I no longer trusted her nor wanted to be around her. My last final was on a Tuesday morning so instead of leaving Thursday as I originally planned, I was taking off today. If I didn't have to stay here a minute longer, I wasn't going to.

I hadn't told anyone I was coming home early. Like always my first stop would be to see Coby. Since I didn't leave West Virginia until after five o'clock it was already starting to get dark outside. I Couldn't wait to see the look on Coby's face when I surprised him with my early arrival. This entire summer I planned on dedicating it to fixing the strained relationship I had created between Coby and me. My main focus would be my man and nothing else. Instead of carrying all my bag inside tonight I would just grab the tomorrow morning. When I put my key in the door, I made sure to open and close it as quietly as possible. I don't want him to hear me, so I tipped toes upstairs and when I heard moaning, I assumed that Coby was watching porn as always. Coby had developed a weird as fascination with porn and as bad as I disliked it that was his thing, so I never said anything. When I busted through the bedroom door, I was immediately sick to my stomach. I couldn't hold in my tears and the food I had earlier for lunch. Witnessing the love of my life balls deep in a fuckin man that looked like a woman crushed me to my soul. If it wasn't for me seeing the long skinny dick hanging low, I would have never known it was another man Coby was fuckin. How could he do this to me, how could I he be in the room he claims we shared fucking someone else another man at that.

"Lee what the fuck are you doing here" Coby yell jumping up from the position he was in. Racing towards me. I hadn't prepared for what was going to happen next because I was still throwing up. More like dry heaving because I had emptied out my stomach when I first opened the door. Instead of explaining himself and consoling me Coby started punching me with all his might and fighting me as if I was a stranger on the street that had just broken into his home. "Why the fuck would you just bust in and pop on me unannounced bitch! You better no mention a word of this to any fucking body do you hear me?" I couldn't even answer his question because I was screaming the top of my lungs for him to stop and get off of me. The he, she Coby was just balls deep in must have felt bad watching him beat the shit out of me because he was now pulling Coby off of me telling him to calm down and stop. I was in any form happy that the "it" was her, but

I was thankful that he was able to save me from the worst ass beating I had got in my entire life. I struggled to get up on my feet and ran to my car. Leaving Coby's front door wide open and not worrying about anything else besides getting the fuck out of there as quick as possible. I was shaken and beaten bloody so I couldn't go to my parents' house. The first person I thought to contact was my sister Renee. I hopped on the nearest freeways to head to her house and it started pouring down raining. As if it wasn't hard enough to see with a swollen eye from Coby's beating, I was crying and attempting to text Renee and let her know I was on my way to her house. I got a text from Coby after hitting send on the message to Renee.

Coby: Just because you left just now doesn't mean you're leaving me Lee, I don't care what you saw or how you feel about this we are not over and If I can't have you then no one will.

Before I could put my phone back between my legs, I heard a loud horn coming from a semi-truck behind me. I tried to swerve back into the lane I was previously in, but it was too late. Being wet and slippery I served and lost control of the wheel. I felt the first hit my car begin to tumble. My head was playing ping pong hitting different areas of my car. I felt another hard impact and my car came to a complete stop but not before the airbag busted through my steering wheel and hit me in the face. Right when I thought the impact was over, I felt an even larger boom and blood trickling down my face "God please help me and..." before I could finish my prayer everything went black.........................

TO BE CONTINUED!